SMALL ACTS OF amazing COURAGE

Gloria Whelan

A PAULA WISEMAN BOOK
SIMON & SCHUSTER BOOKS FOR YOUNG READERS
NEW YORK   LONDON   TORONTO   SYDNEY

SIMON & SCHUSTER BOOKS FOR YOUNG READERS
An imprint of Simon & Schuster Children's Publishing Division
1230 Avenue of the Americas, New York, New York 10020

This book is a work of fiction. Any references to historical events, real people,
or real locales are used fictitiously. Other names, characters, places, and incidents
are products of the author's imagination, and any resemblance to actual events
or locales or persons, living or dead, is entirely coincidental.

SIMON & SCHUSTER BOOKS FOR YOUNG READERS
is a trademark of Simon & Schuster, Inc.
For information about special discounts for bulk purchases,
please contact Simon & Schuster Special Sales at
1-866-506-1949 or business@simonandschuster.com.
The Simon & Schuster Speakers Bureau can bring authors to your live event.
For more information or to book an event, contact the Simon & Schuster Speakers Bureau at
1-866-248-3049 or visit our website at www.simonspeakers.com.
Book design by Lizzy Bromley
The text for this book is set in Bembo and Odette.
Manufactured in the United States of America, 0311 FFG
2 4 6 8 10 9 7 5 3 1
Library of Congress Cataloging-in-Publication Data
Whelan, Gloria.
Small acts of amazing courage / Gloria Whelan.—1st ed.
p. cm.
"A Paula Wiseman Book."
Summary: In 1919, independent-minded Rosalind
lives in India with her English parents, and when they fear she has
fallen in with some rebellious types who believe in Indian
self-government, she is sent "home" to London, where she has never been
before and where her older brother died, to stay with her two aunts.
ISBN 978-1-4424-0931-6 (hardcover)
1. India—History—British occupation, 1765–1947—Juvenile fiction. 2. Great Britain—History—
George V, 1910–1936—Juvenile fiction. [1. London (England)—History—20th century—Juvenile
fiction. 2. India—History—British occupation, 1765–1947—Fiction. 3. London (England)—
History—20th century—Fiction. 4. Great Britain—History—George V, 1910–1936—Fiction.
5. Grief—Fiction. 6. Self-confidence—Fiction. 7. Aunts—Fiction.] I. Title.
PZ7.W5718Sm 2011
[Fic]—dc22
2010013164
ISBN 978-1-4424-0933-0 (eBook)

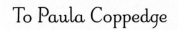

To Paula Coppedge

How can kindness get you into so much trouble? It started when Mother dropped into sickness and I was left on my own. No, before that, when the war came and Father, a major in the British Indian Army who led a battalion of Gurkha Rifles, went off to the war. The battalion was sent to fight in countries I had never heard of and whose names I couldn't spell.

It wasn't as if Mother and I were alone. There were all the servants: gardeners, sweepers, cooks, servers, and Father's *cyce,* his groom, who had nothing to do since Father was away, but out of kindness Mother would not let him go, because he had a family to support. Ranjit was the *burra mali,* the head of all the servants, and Amina was my *ayah,* though at my age I was much too old to have a nursemaid, so Amina was really Mother's lady's maid.

Mother's English friends were often in and out of our house with criticisms of me disguised as kindness. Mrs. Cartwright said, "Rosalind is such an original child. I don't know that I have ever seen a girl's hair worn in quite that way." My hair grows and grows like the leaves on a rain tree. I won't tie it back neatly or wear a band. Worst of all, I go outside in the Indian sun without a hat. Mrs. Cartwright had something to say about that as well. "The sun will turn Rosalind into a regular Indian. Soon you won't be able to tell her from your servants. It's a pity she wasn't sent home." Mother only drew her lips into a straight line to keep from telling Sibil Cartwright to mind her own business.

Though I have never been there, home, of course, is England. India is considered dangerous for children, and the schools here for us English are looked down upon. The minute the Cartwrights' children got to be six years old, they were packed off and sent to live with relatives in England so they could attend proper schools. I heard Mrs. Cartwright reading letters from them to Mother. The dear little things sounded so brave, but you could tell they were miserable away from their mother and father. They described horrible dishes of boiled cabbage and winters so cold they had to wear gloves indoors to keep from getting chilblains.

I should have been suffering in England as well, but luckily Mother refused to let me go. When Father tried to insist, she got all shaky and sobbed, and the doctor had to be sent for. She wouldn't let me go, because the saddest thing in the world had happened. My brother, Edward, who died before I was born, was sent to school in England when he was seven. On vacations from his boarding school he stayed with my mother's two sisters, Aunt Louise and Aunt Ethyl. Neither of the sisters had married. They lived alone in the house left to them by my grandparents.

In Edward's first year at school there was a diphtheria epidemic. Two boys died. Edward was one of them. Mother told me all about it and even showed me the letters Aunt Louise and Aunt Ethyl had sent telling of the sad news— the most tender letter in the world from Aunt Louise, and a mournful letter from Aunt Ethyl that gave much distress and little comfort.

Because he was buried in England, Mother has never even seen his grave. Each year as his birthday comes around she must be content to put flowers in a vase in Edward's room. The room is kept exactly as it was before he went to England. The door to the room is closed, and Amina, who keeps it tidy, is the only one allowed inside, but I have stolen into the room and seen his clothes, his cricket bat, his pictures of England's cricket team, and his teddy bear worn on the ears because he sucked on them. When I was little, I used to think his ghost had come back and lived in there. I was afraid it was angry with me because I had taken my brother's place.

When Father or Mrs. Cartwright talked of the dangers right here in India, dangers like cholera and malaria and typhoid fever, Mother said England was even more dangerous, and look at what happened to Edward. When I came along only a few months after Edward died, she swore she would never let me out of her sight.

Up until now I had not been worried about being sent away. After the war started, there were no ships to take me to England. I had caught myself being almost glad of a war that kept me safe in India. Then I told myself I was hateful, for every day in the *Times of India* there were long columns naming British soldiers who had been killed. What if one day Father's name should appear on the list? I promised

God I would go to England anytime he wanted me to and eat boiled cabbage if he spared Father.

Thank heavens Father, who had been fighting in battles thousands of miles away, had been spared, but he wasn't home yet. Though the war ended in November of 1918, there were violent demonstrations by Indians who wanted their freedom from British rule. The army was needed to put the demonstrations down. But now, six months after the armistice, Mother had received word that Father and his troops would be coming home any day.

Mother was all aflutter with preparations for his return, for without Father to see to things, our house and garden had grown untidy. The house is too large for our small family of three, but because of Father's position before the war, and the position of deputy commissioner he would be returning to, an impressive home was expected of us. The rooms were large and the ceilings high so that the warm air would rise. The floors of stone and tile were cool on bare feet. We lived in a kind of half-light, hardly bright enough to read by, for our windows were always shuttered to keep out the sun.

Everything needed tending to. You could draw pictures on the icing of dust that lay on the furniture. There was sand scrunched into the oriental rugs. In the yard the bougainvillea had overtaken the house, burying it in floods of purple flowers.

To prepare for Father's return, Ranjit chased the servants into sweeping and scrubbing, shaking his fist so hard when he found a missed bit of sand or dirt that his *pugree,* his turban, would slip onto the side of his head. The *chota mali,* the little assistant gardener, laughed to see it, making Ranjit shout angry words and speak with disrespect of the *chota mali*'s mother, for Ranjit prized his dignity above all else.

All the running about and shouting flurried Mother, who has what she calls a lazy heart, so that Dr. Morton had to be sent for. He came with his black bag, which was never out of his hand. When I was very young, I thought it a part of him like the elephant's trunk. He listened to her heartbeat and told Mother she must rest. So she lay in her room all day on her chaise longue, with the shutters closed against the sun. The little bearer brought her glasses of *nimbu-pani,* fresh lime juice, on a silver tray with a spray of sweet-smelling jasmine he had picked himself. The bearer was only twelve, but he was half in love with Mother, who was at her most beautiful in her rose-colored silk dressing gown with her hair arranged by Amina into a pile of gold.

Of course I was excited about Father's return, but all the cleaning was a great nuisance, for I had to have my room turned out and all my special things disturbed and dusted roughly—my butterfly collection, my first kite, the crocodile tooth, and the pot of kohl my friend Isha showed me how to use. When I was alone, I painted the kohl around my eyes and made them look immense, like the bits of blue glass ringed round with black lead in the church window. Though I pleaded with him not to, Ranjit also carried away the four feet of snakeskin a viper had rubbed off on the stones around our fountain.

To get away from all the busyness, I went in search of Isha. Isha is Amina's daughter. We were raised together. Shortly after Amina was hired to be my *ayah,* Mother learned Amina had a daughter of her own. Having just lost Edward, Mother could not bear for Amina to be separated all day from her child, so Isha was put in the nursery with me. Father was angry, saying it was unsuitable for me to be so close to an Indian baby. But since it was only a few months after Edward's death, Father found he was no match for Mother's tears. After that, Isha was always in the nursery with me. I learned Hindi from her, and she learned

English from me. When we talked, it was in a scramble of the two languages, though Mother cautioned me never to use a Hindi word in Father's hearing or he would forbid me to play with Isha.

When I started school, I saw less and less of her for, of course, like most Indian girls, she did not go to school, and Father saw that my time was spent with girls from other English families, girls who were boring as Isha never was. After Father left for the war and Mother took to the chaise longue, forgetting to keep track of me, I once again began to spend time with Isha. Our favorite thing was to go together to the bazaar. Though like me Isha was only fifteen, she was a *biwi,* a wife. Her husband, Aziz Mertha, was much older than she was and left her to herself, asking only that she help his mother, Mrs. Mertha, in the housework and the preparation of meals and that many more babies would come.

Aziz spent his days in the bazaar, where he worked in the stall of a merchant who sold rare ivory carvings and rugs so old their colors were like memories of color. There was something else about Isha's husband. Sometimes when we were in the bazaar we saw men stop at his stall, and there was talk so quiet that even if you were close you could not hear what was being said. At those times Isha hurried me away. When I asked whom the men were, she only said, "Aziz won't tell me, but they belong to something called the Congress Party. He talks all the time of how India must be free to rule itself."

"You mean India would fight us British?"

"No. He wants no wars and no violence. It is a great secret, but a famous man named Gandhi came to our house. When he wants the British to give India a scrap of freedom, Gandhi stops eating until he gets his way. The British are afraid he will die and upset all the Indians, so they give in. Gandhi says nonviolence like that is greater than all the force of arms."

I wanted to know about a man who could get his way by refusing to eat, but Isha would say no more.

Mother warned me never to go to the bazaar. It is not done for an English girl to be seen there, and she knows how upset Father would be. She found out about my being there from Mrs. Cartwright, who told Mother I had been in the bazaar with an Indian girl. Mother knew at once that it was Isha. She called me into her room and had me sit on the chaise, then took my hand and shed tears, saying she didn't know how she was expected to run the house without Father and make do with all the shortages because of the war and look after me as well. Mother made me tie back my hair, clean my nails, put on a clean dress, and promise never to go outside without my *topee,* my pith helmet, a sort of upside-down bowl-shaped helmet that protected you from the sun. Though Mother and I both hated their ugliness, Father always insisted that we wear ours when we were1 out of doors. As far as I'm concerned, *topees* were invented to keep people's thoughts imprisoned inside their head. Heaven forbid anyone should say what they really thought.

Mother said, "And something more, Rosalind. Just because school is out doesn't mean you should abandon your education. Why don't you sit in the garden and read a book?" She gave me some of the books from the club library. I loved all the books by Dickens, but a lot of the books were slushy stories. I read Isha the parts where the characters made love, and Isha said it wasn't at all like that.

Isha lived on the outskirts of our property among a tumble of servants' huts. When I visited her, I always thought about how much our servants knew about us and how little we knew about them. They are a great mystery.

I saw how miserable it was for them, for it was May, the hottest month of the year, with the cooling rains of the monsoon a month away. In the trees the common hawk-cuckoo, which we called the brainfever bird because of its irritating call, screeched endlessly. The servants' huts were little and cramped, no larger than one of the smaller rooms in our house. The floors were dirt, and when the rains seeped in, mud. The sun beat on the iron roofs and there was nothing but *tattys,* screens of woven grass soaked in water, to keep out the heat and mosquitoes. Worst of all, there wasn't enough room to ever be alone. In our house we had high ceilings, thick walls, shutters to close out the sun, and electric fans. There were cool drinks with ice, and if you liked, you could be in a room all by yourself.

Mrs. Mertha was busy in the courtyard with some other women. I sneaked into the Merthas' hut, smelling the spicy smell that lingered from all the meals. Isha was crushing cardamom seeds for their dinner and singing her favorite *raga,* a song about two lovers who were separated by cruel parents. She was as anxious to escape to the bazaar as I was. Her mother-in-law was not satisfied with anything that Isha did and was angry with Isha that no baby had come. "She feeds me horrible-tasting herbs to help me become pregnant," Isha said, "when it is not my fault at all but that of Aziz, who is too lazy to do what he should."

To be seen to advantage in the bazaar, Isha put on her best *sari* with its matching *choli*. They were a beautiful pinky peach color and made her look like a ripe mango. Her eyes were outlined with kohl, and her hair was neatly braided and shiny from the coconut oil she had rubbed into it. The part was dusted with vermillion powder, and like the red *tikka,* the red dot on her forehead, this was meant to signify she was a married woman. Beside her I looked washed out and dull, like the faded photographs of past members that hung on the club walls.

The bazaar was on a bank that overlooked the river. The river is the most important thing about our town, and like all rivers in India that flow into or out of the holy Ganges River, it is sacred. Everywhere you looked on the river, something was happening. In the morning people came to wash and to brush their teeth with twigs. Later in the day women, with their *saris* tucked up out of the way, beat clothes with sticks to get the clothes clean. A steamer carrying mail sailed into port. The fishermen were out in their dhows, the patched sails billowing in the wind. There were prows with eyes painted on them, the better to see where they were going. Some families even made their home on boats, and I thought how much I would like that. A heron flew by, neck bent into an S shape, legs dragging. Wild dogs, their bones as much outside as inside their skinny bodies, lapped water. A young boy might ride his water buffalo right into the river and then proceed to give him a cooling bath. A procession of mourners would march down the *ghat,* each step a new cause for sorrowful cries. A fire would be built and the body burned. In a day or so, when all the burning was over, the relatives would return to gather the ashes and put them into the river. Sometimes the ashes from the funeral pyres blew into the bazaar, sifting down on me so that I felt the dead had become a part of me. I had seen the bodies of babies sent down the river on little rafts covered in marigold blooms. The sick came to bathe for health. The river was like a great pair of arms taking everyone and everything in and giving comfort.

Isha and I dodged a bullock cart and a wandering cow followed by a woman who was picking up the cowpats to mix with rice straw. The mess would be dried and used as fuel for cooking fires. There was so much to see at the bazaar. The monkey man was putting on a show with his two trained monkeys. A man split coconuts in half with a great cleaver and sold the juice. There was a talking mynah bird for sale. Another man with a kind of mangle pressed sugarcane into a sweet juice. There were mounds of bright pink watermelon sherbet. A *sadhu,* a holy man, sat cross-legged, meditating, his long beard wagging as he prayed. I loved the way I could walk through the bazaar and own all the beautiful things with my eyes. We paused at a stall to look longingly at the bolts of cloth in rainbow colors that would be turned into *saris,* some of them embroidered with gold thread. There was a stall hung with brightly colored kites, and another with garlands of orange marigolds. One stall was all pots and pans, and another, piles of fragrant cardamom, turmeric, and pepper. But there was also the stink of open drains and the *bidis,* the hand-rolled cigarettes that everyone smoked.

There were pitiful beggars as well, men and women missing fingers and noses from leprosy, blind people, and people with elephantiasis whose legs and feet were swollen. The very worst of all were the children who, when they were babies, had had the soft bones of their arms and legs twisted and misshapen so you would be sorry for them and fill their begging bowls.

There was a frightening man with disheveled hair, black clothes, and an evil look who came every day. One of his eyes was sealed shut, and the other eye stared hard when he looked at you, as if it were making up for the eye that couldn't see. Isha and I called him the Cobra. The Cobra arrived each morning with three crippled children in a cart. He placed them with their bowls at strategic locations in the bazaar, and then late in the day he would gather them up like so many dolls that had lost their stuffing and take them away along with all they had earned for him.

Isha always dropped a few *paise* into their bowls. Often she scolded me. "You must have a lot of money, living in that big house. Why don't you give? Why are you so selfish?"

The truth was, Mother was a poor manager and we were always short of money. Often the servants had to wait for their wages. "I don't know where the money goes," Mother would complain. "Your Father always took care of those things." She would turn to Ranjit, who would show her in his books just where every *rupee* was spent. Mother would see waste here and there and promise to be more careful, but the next month it would be the same.

The only money I had was the shiny shilling I got each

Christmas from my Aunt Louise in England. This Christmas, along with the shilling, there was the usual cheery note:

My very dear Rosy,

I have your picture here before me as I write, but the picture is of a seven-year-old, and surely you must have changed a bit. I suppose your two front teeth have grown in and your hair is no longer in braids. I know with your father away, you are the light of your mother's life and the dear smile I see in the picture before me is cheering her days.

All my love,
Aunt Louise

P.S. Please spend this shilling on something that is as foolish as it is fun!

Aunt Ethyl sent me flannel bellybands and a greasy cream to smear on my face to keep it from darkening in the sun. Her gifts were accompanied by a less pleasant note:

Dear Rosalind,

I am sorry that you have been so negligent in writing. Even if writing to me is an unpleasant task, as I gather from your reluctance it must be, one would hope good manners would prevail and you would be more regular in your correspondence.

I trust you are staying out of the sun and eschewing any of the indigestible highly spiced local food. One must observe moderation in all things.

Sincerely,
Aunt Ethyl

Aunt Ethyl's flannel bellybands were scrunched away in the back of my dresser drawer. I still had Aunt Louise's shilling. I had shown it to Isha, but I was saving it until next Christmas, when I got another shilling, and then I would spend it. As long as I had the one shilling, I could imagine buying a great many things, so that I felt they were nearly mine. The minute I spent the shilling, there would be no more possibilities.

That day at Aziz's stall there were Turkish rugs in soft blues and reds, silver teapots, and lovely enameled vases. Isha told me that they had belonged to one of the British families, the Livingstones, who were in trouble and had needed to sell all their pretty things. The Livingstones were friends of Mother and Father's and lived just down the cantonment from us. The cantonment is where all of us British live. Mr. Livingstone oversaw the railways, but Isha whispered that one of his servants had told her Mr. Livingstone spent most of his time at the club drinking, and now he was going to be replaced and sent in disgrace back to England.

I felt sorry for him and said so, but Isha shrugged. "*Baap* says he beats his servants. Let's see how he likes it in England when he has to do his own dirty work." Servants in India were very cheap, and we all had them. But friends of Mother and Father's who had gone home wrote that in England servants were so dear you could only have one, or at best, two.

Late in the afternoon, the smell of the vendors' food, the *jelabis* and *samosas,* reminded Isha that she must go home to help in the preparation of dinner. I followed her out of the bazaar and along the dusty road, where she turned into the busy village of servants' huts, leaving me to straggle down the path that led to home, where I found Mother waiting for me. "I have just heard," she said, putting her arms around me and surprising me with a hug, "that tomorrow your father will be home."

Father had been away for two years, so I was shy of the tall man with the dark tan who strode into our house and gathered me into his arms, hugging me so fiercely the brass buttons on his uniform dug into my chest. He had grown a mustache, and I wasn't used to its bristly tickle. After Mother's gentle caresses, the strength of his hug took away my breath. Father looked and looked as if he could not get enough of me. "Rosy," he said, calling me by his pet name for me, "you've grown into a fine young woman."

He began to stride about the house and garden. "You can't know how I longed for this day," he said. "At night

I would put myself to sleep by imagining myself walking from room to room, through the drawing room with the shutters closed against the sun, through my study with my favorite books and the dining room set for our dinner, you and your mother there at the table, you telling me all the things you had done that day, and afterwards all of us in the garden with the hibiscus and oleander in blossom and the sound of the water falling from the fountain." He smiled at us. "Even now, I have to touch everything to be sure it's not my imagination."

Father had brought us presents. He gave mother a ring set with an emerald just the color of her eyes, and for me he had a necklace of cleverly carved ivory beads. For Amina there was a silk scarf and for Ranjit a walking stick in bright wood, which he immediately began to use to prod the *chota mali* into working faster.

Mother and I could hardly let Father out of our sight. We went together to see a welcome-home parade of the Second Battalion of the Gurkha Rifles, which Father commanded. Father was regal in his uniform, with its rows of brightly colored ribbons, and the Indian *havildars*, who were noncommissioned officers, and *sepoys*, who were privates, looked suitably impressive in their starched blue uniforms and their bright blue and gold turbans. The whole town, English and Indian, turned out and cheered wildly.

Mother was better now that Father had returned, and there were few afternoons on the chaise. She began to plan parties to welcome Father and to go to parties given for the other officers who, like Father, were home from the war. Our house, where it seemed that we had been tiptoeing about forever, was now full of people laughing and chattering.

When there was no company and I could get Father to myself, I begged for stories of the war. Father's battalion had fought the Turks, who were on the side of the Germans and against England. The battles had taken place in Meso-potamia, near the Tigris River. Father spun the globe that always sat on his desk and put his finger on the exact spot. "We were at the very place where the Garden of Eden was supposed to have been," Father said, "but it was more hell than paradise."

There was a lot he would not tell me about the war. His feelings seemed to close in on him as if he were slamming shut a book. All he said was, "Those Turks were devils with a bayonet." The Gurkha soldiers in Father's battalion came from Nepal, a country north of India high in the Himalayas. "You can't find braver men," Father said. "They crossed that river with the Turks firing away at them and never looked back. This country should be proud that its own people helped to protect the British Empire. Unfortunately, there were a few Indian men who fought not with us but with the Turks, against us."

"Why did they do that?" I asked.

"They had some misguided idea of independence from England, after all England has done for them. And just see what it led to: the terrible tragedy in Amritsar."

"What happened in Amritsar?" I asked, wanting to know his version, for Isha had whispered to me that in the city of Amritsar, thousands of Indians had gathered to celebrate a festival. The British army believed the Indian people were there not to celebrate but to demonstrate against British rule. The soldiers had been ordered to shoot, and hundreds of Indians had died.

Father said, "A brigadier general lost his head. I suppose he thought the gathering of Indians was a bunch of Bolsheviks. It was very nasty and best forgotten." He would say no more.

The magic of Father's return was soon over for him, and he began to look at our home in a different way. I could see he was trying not to be critical, that he was making an effort to be patient with Mother and me, but there were long sessions with Ranjit. He ordered dead trees cut and new ones planted. He examined the storeroom, which should have been locked at all times and its key with Mother, but Mother had often handed the key to cook or one of the other servants in need of supplies. Father found a great difference between what was on the list and the dwindling tins of marmalade and sardines and biscuits, all things especially precious because they had not been available from England during the war. "There has been carelessness," Father said. Carelessness was something Father could not stand.

He conferred with Ranjit on every one of the servants, asking exactly what they did and what was paid to them. "Why do we have two sweepers?" he demanded. The sweepers are outcastes and are considered the lowest of the low among the Hindus. It was their job to sweep the house and garden paths and to empty the chamber pots. The Hindus in India have a caste system so that everyone knows what their standing is. Isha says first there are the priests, then the warriors and rulers, and then the merchants and farmers. After that are the laborers. The poor outcastes belong to no caste at all.

Ranjit said, "The sweeper, Jetha, who has been with us all these years, has a little trouble with the work. He is getting old. I hired a young sweeper to help him."

"If he is too old for the work, let him go."

A frown appeared on Ranjit's forehead. "But, Sahib, Jetha has always been with us. He has a large family of children and grandchildren who depend on even his small wage."

Father was firm. "It's time they found work for themselves and took care of Jetha for a change."

"Sahib, Jetha is a sweeper, as are all his family. The other Hindus will not hire them. They are considered unclean."

"That's Hindu nonsense and has nothing to do with me. Get rid of him." In that way several of the servants departed and a few younger ones were hired on. Mother was admonished never to give the key to the stores to anyone but Ranjit, and more sardines and marmalade were ordered from England.

"It is a miracle that things were not worse," Father said. "I give the credit to Ranjit. In spite of my not being here, he has managed very well. Without him the house would have fallen apart."

When the house was put in order, it was my turn.

Father called me into his study and plucked a book from the shelves, handed it to me, and asked me to read to him. The book was Tennyson's *Idylls of the King*. It was a book I had read many times because it was all about King Arthur and Guinevere, but it was also about poor, sad Queen Victoria and the death of her husband, Prince Albert. At first I read slowly and enunciated carefully as Father always instructed me to, but then I came to these words:

> *"Break not, O woman's-heart, but still endure;*
> *Break not, for thou art Royal, but endure,*
> *Remembering all the beauty of that star*
> *Which shone so close beside Thee that ye made*
> *One light together, but has past and leaves*
> *The Crown a lonely splendor."*

I lost myself in the words and rushed on until Father stopped me.

"Just as I thought," he said. "You are picking up a Hindi accent." He appeared very cross.

"But, Father," I said, "the Westons hired a governess from France just so their children could have a French accent."

"Don't be pert, Rosalind. That's not the same thing at all. We must do something about that. You are spending too much time here with the servants and picking up their accent. Why aren't you at the club with the other English children?"

Father must have known that Mother had not been well enough to take me to the club, and even if I could have gone on my own, I wouldn't have. The leftover children— that is, the ones who had not been sent to England before the war—were so dull. Amy Weston, who was my age and went to school with me, stood there with this stupid smile until you noticed her dress and told her how pretty it was. Once, when I confided to her that I sometimes went to the bazaar, she looked at me as if I were very strange. She sat on the club's porch sipping lemonade and hoping one of the young soldiers who were home on leave would notice her. I was relieved that Mother didn't take me to the club and that instead I had Isha and the exciting world of the bazaar, but of course I didn't tell Father that.

"I must have your mother organize a little get-together for you with some other girls your age. And what have you learned at school?" He quizzed me on my French and Latin and math and then gave a great sigh. "It's a pity that you did not go to England for your schooling." He was silent for a moment, and then he said, as if he were one person telling something to another person, and I was not there, "Ships have resumed sailing again to England. It's not too late."

Immediately I saw myself put in chains and slung into the hold of a ship. Of course I knew it would not be like that, but the thought of leaving India and Mother and Father and our home felt that way. Father saw the look on my face and hastily said, "Never mind. Now that I am home we'll sort things out, but I don't like the rumors I hear of you having been seen in the bazaar. That is totally unacceptable."

I guessed that Father had spoken to Mother about me and even mentioned England, for Mother was very pale and took to her chaise. She had me come and read to her so that she might keep an eye on me, lest Father sneak me away while she wasn't looking and ship me off to the dreaded England.

The next day Mother accompanied me to the club. There were always complicated preparations for these occasions. Even in the hot days of an Indian summer Mother had me put on long silk stockings, a garter belt, and a slip that clung to my body like a leech. The collar of my dress chafed my neck, and by the time I had dressed I was damp with perspiration. For once Mother seemed not to mind the heat, and in her flowered voile dress and her hat that bloomed a silk rose, she looked like a bouquet. Even her white gloves had tiny rosebuds on them. We motored to the club in our ancient Packard, which had survived the war. Ashok, our driver, kept his hand on the horn as he urged the auto through bicycles, oxcarts, horse *tongas,* stray cows, and the crowds of people that were everywhere. Because of the dust, the car windows were shut tightly and the inside of the car was hellishly hot. I felt the wetness under my armpits and on the back of my dress. Mother kept putting her hand over her eyes as Ashok barely missed running down the small children who walked alongside the car pounding on the windows and begging for coins.

When at last we were safe inside the club it seemed a little cooler with the green lawn, flowerbeds, and a sky blue pool with children swimming about sending up sprays of water, and everywhere vases of blooms for the day before the women had their flower show. The clubhouse was divided into a party room for dances, a large comfortable room for the men where they played billiards and had their own dining room hung with photographs of winning tennis and cricket teams and an imposing portrait of our king, George V, and a smaller, much less grand section for women with a bridge room and a small parlor with a tatty sofa and wicker chairs left over from a redo of the men's section.

Mother's friends Mrs. Cartwright and Mrs. Weston, who were so critical of the way I wore my hair and went out in the sun, were there with another woman. The three of them were sitting in the parlor, their skirts trembling in the breezes from the electric fans, and sipping tall glasses of something iced. They waved mother over and I trailed along, unsure of what else to do.

"Well, stranger," Mrs. Cartwright said to Mother, "how nice to see you. We've missed you, and of course Rosalind as well, although I suspect she has had more interesting things to do." I was standing close to Mother and felt her stiffen, remembering how Mrs. Cartwright had reported seeing me at the bazaar.

Mrs. Weston said, "Your Rosalind is such an interesting child. I'm afraid my Amy is happy just to do the things ordinary girls are expected to do."

The third woman, whom I hadn't seen before, was listening to these comments with a secret smile on her face. She was the only woman in the club without a hat, and even more shocking, a quick glance at her ankles, which could be seen thrust out from an old-fashioned long skirt, told me she was bare legged. Now she said to Mother and to me, "Sit down, my dears, and let us order something cool for you. I want to hear more about this interesting child. The ordinary can get a bit boring."

I immediately loved her, but Mrs. Weston flushed. I think she would have liked to make an angry reply, but she ignored the remark and instead said to me, "Rosalind, my dear, why don't you go and find Amy."

Amy, who went to my school, was sitting by the pool in the shade of an umbrella with another girl. I saw that my dressy clothes were all wrong for the hot afternoon, for the girls were both in their bathing suits with towels draped over their shoulders, and they wore large straw boaters with ribbons hanging down. Amy's blond hair was curled in a becoming style that must have taken ages to do. The other girl was what people call plain; that is, she was everything you would expect and nothing surprising. The two of them were talking together, but their attention was on three young lieutenants sitting across the pool from them. When two of the lieutenants got up and disappeared into the men's dressing room, Amy turned her attention to me and, indicating the other girl, said, "Sarah Harvey." To Sarah she said, "Rosalind James," making my name sound like something on a list of insects to be avoided. I settled onto an empty chair.

"You're dressed for a tea party," Sarah said. "Where is your bathing suit?"

Before I could answer, Amy said, "I was telling Sarah that now that the war is over, I'll be going to England. I expect I'll be presented at court." She gave me a critical look. "I don't suppose you want to go to England," she said.

"No," I said. "I don't."

To Sarah she said, "Rosalind wouldn't want to leave her friends." Amy made the word *friends* sound odious, and I guessed there was talk of my having been seen with Isha.

I couldn't help myself. I said, "I think you have to be someone really important to be presented at court. Anyhow, you have to wear feathers in your hair, and I think that's ridiculous."

"No more ridiculous than putting red powder in your hair."

So she did mean Isha.

"I don't know what you two are talking about," Sarah

said, "but if I went, I'd have to stay with my grandparents, and they live off in the country and there's nothing around them. It wouldn't be like London, with so much to do. And it's freezing in the winter."

"I'll have a fur coat," Amy said. "And my uncle *is* important. He's something in the government, and he has a lot to say about India. He wrote to my parents that all this talk about India breaking away from England and becoming independent was very dangerous. He said Indian people who belong to the Congress Party would be arrested if they aren't careful."

"What do you mean?" I asked, thinking of Isha's husband, Aziz.

Amy said, "The Congress Party wants all us English to go home."

"I thought you *wanted* to go back to England," I said.

"That's different. It's not like I want the Indians to take over the country." She gave me a withering look. "Anyone who knows anything would have nothing to do with Indians. They're against England."

Sarah said, "Mrs. Nelson has Indians to parties at her house all the time."

"Who is Mrs. Nelson?" I asked.

"She's the woman who's sitting with our mothers." Amy said. "Her husband is the head of a large jute company."

I remember Father telling me once that jute that came from plant fibers was the way planters in this part of India made their living. We often saw boats on the river carrying bales of jute to be sold and turned into rope.

Amy said, "She's a little strange, but everyone has to be nice to her because her husband practically owns the town. He's really rich and they have a big house, but you'd never know it from the way Mrs. Nelson dresses. With her money she could get all her clothes from Paris."

Sarah said, "You don't see her here very often. She runs some kind of orphanage for Indian children."

Mrs. Nelson was forgotten when two of the three lieutenants came strolling out of the men's dressing room and dove into the water with a huge splash. A few drops landed on us. When they emerged, Amy called to them, "You nearly drowned us!"

"Come on in and you can drown us!" one of the men answered. Giggling, Sarah and Amy threw off their hats and the towels they had draped around their shoulders, then climbed into the pool, careful not to get their hair wet.

Left to myself, I was about to wander back to Mother when the third lieutenant walked over. After asking if he might join me, he collapsed on a chair and stuck out his long legs. His uniform appeared to be a size too large, so I guessed he had lost weight. There was a yellow cast to his dark tan, and his brown hair had been clipped close to his head, giving him a skinned look. He couldn't have been more than twenty.

"It looks like you and I have been deserted," he said. "I'm Max Nelson, by the way."

"I'm Rosalind James. Is Mrs. Nelson your mother?"

"Yes, and if we're talking families, is your father Major James by any chance?"

"He is. Do you know him?"

"I was privileged to serve under him."

"So you got to go to Mesopotamia. That must have been so interesting."

"It was terrifying. Land of the ancient Assyrians, you know."

"The poem about them always makes me shiver," I said, and recited, "'The Assyrian came down like the wolf on the fold, / And his cohorts were gleaming in purple and gold.'"

"Good girl," he said. "You know your Byron."

"I always wondered what cohorts were."

"A group of warriors. The Assyrians were a fierce lot, one war after another, chasing whole populations from their lands, building gorgeous palaces with their loot. One of their kings said, 'I built a city with the labors of the peoples subdued by my hand.' *That* makes me shiver. It was all very biblical: Nineveh and Babylon. But they had their own gods: Ishtar, Shamash, Anu, and Ea."

"How do you know so much about Assyria? You must have been too busy fighting to do much reading."

"I was studying history at Cambridge. As soon as I was old enough to enlist, I jumped in. I thought I'd make a little of my own history, but I never figured out what England was doing chasing the Turks around in the land of the Assyrians."

"And will you go back to Cambridge?"

"Yes, at the end of summer. Dad would like me to stay here and take over the business, but I'm going back to King's College with a little more knowledge of history than I had when I left."

I told him, "I have two aunts in England, the Hartley sisters who live on Lord North Street. Isn't that a wonderful name for a street? After you finish your studies, will you return to India?" I tried to hide the hope in my voice.

"Not to run the jute business." He lowered his voice. "Mother says England should give India its freedom, and I agree. I am interested in the Congress Party and one of the party's leaders, a man called Gandhi who is against violence, which is fine with me. I've had enough killing to last a lifetime."

I was anxious to let him know that I had heard all about the Congress Party and Gandhi. I said, "The husband of my friend Isha, Aziz Mertha, has meetings at his parents' house, and once Gandhi was actually there."

Max looked at me with interest. "So you know about Aziz. If you don't want him to get into trouble, you had better keep that information to yourself. Aziz takes a great risk, but Gandhi is an extraordinary man. I think he's a great leader, and when I return to Cambridge I mean to write about him. He studied in England when he was a young man, but people there don't really know how amazing he is. I've only heard him speak once, but I'll never forget it. He says nonviolence must have its roots in love and in the end must lead to friendship with the enemy. What an attractive message that is to someone who has been fighting a war, and not only a war, but seen killings right here in India."

"You mean what happened in Amritsar?"

"Yes, but Gandhi doesn't want revenge for that. He wants justice."

"If he ever comes here again, will you let me know so I can hear him speak too?"

Suddenly, Mrs. Cartwright was standing over us. "I think your Mother is ready to go home, Rosalind," she said. "The heat is a little too much for her."

I suspected it was boredom more than heat. I stood up, and so did Max. "Thank you for the history lesson," I said, and held out my hand.

"I won't forget your request," he replied.

When we were a little way from him, Mrs. Cartwright said, "I wouldn't have too much to do with that boy. A lot of his ideas are nonsense. He gets them from his mother. I can't think what a woman in her position is doing with such radical opinions. Mr. Nelson should have a talk with her."

"What is Mr. Nelson like?" I asked.

"He's always traveling from one jute plantation to another. I don't see that boy working hard enough to make the money his father has."

"Perhaps Max isn't interested in jute."

"Of course, one mightn't be interested in jute, but certainly one should be interested in money."

On the way out, Mrs. Nelson smiled at me as if we shared a secret, and said, "One of these days you must come and visit the children at my orphanage."

3

Mother and Father were dining at the commissioner's house, so I had a tray of cold chicken and rice on the veranda. After supper, I went into the garden, hoping for coolness from the fountain. The sound of the water spilling was refreshing. I had just settled down on a bench and was breathing in the fragrance of the gardenia bushes and admiring a peacock that had spread its tail like an artist making a painting when a little bearer who did errands for Father and Mother ran up to me and plucked at my arm.

He made a proper *namaste* and said, "Missy Sahib, Isha say come quick and bring your shilling."

I was still under the lieutenant's spell. It didn't seem fair that men had all the adventures. I ran to my room, dug among my handkerchiefs where I kept the shilling, and hurried back outside. The bearer scampered through the dusty footpaths as cleverly as a squirrel, leading me to a place on the outskirts of the bazaar. Stalls were set up there by seedy merchants selling used clothes and battered pots and pans and every kind of shabby rubbish that even the most unfortunate would have little use for. I had never been in this section of the bazaar, nor had I been anywhere by myself at such a late hour. The sinking sun darkened the sky, and smoke from the dung fires made everything hazy. There were the sparks of fireflies in the bushes, and somewhere in the distance the rhythm of a drum. A crowd of crows chattered on the top of a neem tree, and bats were already out and arrowing among the stalls.

The little bearer disappeared, and there was no Isha. A stallkeeper with a long grizzled beard and eyebrows so thick I couldn't see his eyes called to me to look at his wares. Some chattering monkeys in a nearby tree dropped down to a low branch, and I could see their ugly faces only inches from mine. As I turned to hurry back home, someone grabbed my arm and I screamed.

Gloria Whelan

"Do you have your shilling?" It was Isha.

"Yes. Do you need money?"

"No, it's for the baby."

"What baby?" The man in the stall was staring at us, a smile on his face, as if he saw profit in our troubles.

In a rush of words urgently whispered, Isha said, "My father told me the Cobra has bought the little grandson of Jetha."

"The sweeper sold his grandson?"

"Ranjit fired him. The father is starving."

"Why don't the other servants help?" But I knew the answer. They had no money to spare, and besides, the baby came from an outcaste family.

"My father said the Cobra paid four *annas* for the baby. You know what the Cobra will do to the baby. To make him a beggar, he'll twist his little legs so he won't be able to walk. Your shilling is worth eight *annas*. For your shilling he'll give the child to you."

I couldn't bear to think of the child in such cruel hands. I showed Isha the shilling, carefully shielding it from the stallkeeper's vision. "Do you know where the Cobra lives?"

"He lives beneath the bridge. You must ask for Pandy. That's the name he is known by."

"I'll follow you."

"No, I must hurry home." She drew her *sari* over her face as if she were already disappearing. "Aziz's mother will be furious with me for slipping away. She never loses a chance to call me lazy and worthless."

"But I thought you would take the baby."

"No, that's not possible. What would Aziz's mother say!"

"Wouldn't your mother take the baby?" No one was kinder than Amina.

"The child of a sweeper? It would pollute our family! But you must hurry before he hurts the baby. And, Rosalind, don't tell anyone it was my idea. My mother-in-law would beat me for concerning myself with a sweeper's child." The next minute, Isha was gone.

I was anxious to escape the stallkeeper's cat-watching-a-bird stare. I knew the bridge that crossed over a small branch of the river, for you had to cross it on your way to the club. It was in one of the poorest sections of the village. Even safe in a car with the windows rolled up, you were glad when you had pulled away and were clear of the bridge and the many beggars who clung like spiders to the car. I felt conspicuous in my Western clothes and wished

I had a *sari* to disappear into, and yet I knew that however out of place I looked, my Western clothes protected
me, for no one would risk harming me, bringing down
the force of the British authorities. Still, every step led me
closer to the parts of the river that frightened me. In the
distance I heard the drumming of *tablas*. Vultures glided
over the towers of silence where the Parsis exposed their
dead. When the vultures were finished, nothing but bones
would remain.

A black cormorant that had been diving for fish
suddenly shot into the air in a flurry of feathers, and a
crocodile surfaced where the bird had been. They said
crocodiles didn't like bright colors, and I wished I had
worn my less noticeable dark blue dress. The shadow
of a jackal disappeared around a deserted shack. When
I came to the bridge, I saw what I had never noticed
before, a small village of huts crowded together on the
shore beneath the bridge's shelter. As I approached the
huts, I saw they were put together with bits of cardboard,
sheets of metal, and tatters of canvas. Were they not under
the protection of the bridge, a hard rain would turn the
shacks into rubbish.

My eyes stung from the smoke of cooking. Women in

shabby *saris* were tending the fires. Naked children, thin from the hookworm they got from running barefoot, were gathered in small groups, too hungry and weak to play together. Where I stood under the darkness of the bridge, a row of squatting men stared out at me. I wanted to escape, but the sight of the small children kept me there, for I couldn't help thinking of what the Cobra planned to do to Jetha's grandchild. I told myself that because it was my father who had turned Jetha out, I had a responsibility to take care of Jetha's baby. I made myself approach one of the women and say "Pandy" as clearly as I could, but the woman seemed terrified by my approach and hid her face with a ragged bit of her *sari*.

An old woman who overheard me indicated one of the huts. "Pandy," she said, and then, in a dialect I didn't understand, she spoke a lot of words that sounded like curses, after which she spit on the ground.

By now all eyes were following me as I moved toward the hut the woman had pointed out. It took several minutes before I could gather the courage to look inside. When I did I saw three small children with twisted limbs huddled together in front of a bowl of rice. They were the beggar children from the bazaar. The bowl was full when I entered the hut, but in seconds the children emptied it as if I meant to take it from them. Looking deeper into the darkness of the hut, which was lit by a wick floating in a saucer of oil, I could see a girl my age. She was so thin, she was hardly there. In her arms she held a naked baby boy who looked to be five or six months old. Its weight was almost too much for her. Behind me I heard an angry shout, and I turned to see the Cobra only inches from me. He shouted in Hindi, "Why are you in my house?" I could smell his foul breath and feel drops of his saliva settle on my face.

I turned to run away, but he was blocking the entrance. Taking a deep breath, I said in my faltering Hindi, "I have come to buy the baby." I showed him my shilling and pointed to the baby. I winced at his touch as he snatched the shilling from my hand. I grabbed the baby from the girl, who was too weak to offer any resistance. I had never held a baby, and I was surprised at its weight. I suppose I had thought a baby would be like a doll, something easy to handle and toss about. Instead it was solid in my arms. I felt it sink against me as if it had found a familiar place.

I tried to push past the Cobra. He wouldn't move, but only stood there staring at the shilling in his hand. Suddenly, he reached out for the baby. I don't know where I found the courage, but I knew I would never allow the baby back in his hands. I shouldered him aside and ran out of the hut, shoving my way through the crowd of men and women gathered to see what was going on. I kept running, the baby clasped to my chest, its heavy warmth strangely comforting.

I didn't stop until I was safely on our property, but now there was another trouble. What if I were seen with the baby? There had been no time for a plan. If I gave the baby back to the sweeper, it might be sold again. I couldn't go to Mother or Father with an Indian baby in my arms. They would be furious with me for venturing into so dangerous a place and meddling with Indian matters. They would turn out the sweeper's family from their hut in the servants' village. I couldn't go to Ranjit or Amina, for as Isha said, they would have nothing to do with a sweeper's baby. I hid myself in the oleander bushes, breathing in the fragrance of its pink flowers and trying to think what to do. The baby reached out its small hand to pluck one of the flowers. Alarmed, I darted out of the shrubbery, for as a child I had been warned over and over that every part of an oleander bush was deadly and would poison me.

Here was something new. Responsibility. I had never been responsible for another human being. Suppose the baby had put the flower in his mouth. My carelessness could have caused his death. All my life, my first thought had been of me; now all that had changed, and I had to think first of the child in my arms.

It was dark now, and the lights from our house shone through the shutters. One of the *malis* left the house to return to the servants' compound. The beam from the lantern he carried brushed me for a moment, but he didn't see me. It would be another hour or more before Mother and Father returned from the party at the commissioner's home. I pushed open a shutter and crept into a passageway at the back of the house that led to Edward's room. It seemed exactly the right place for the baby. For just a moment I imagined Mother's and Father's happiness at finding a little boy alive and well in the room that had been so unhappy a place. The next moment I was filled with misgiving, worrying that my parents would be angry with me for even stepping foot into the room. When I was little, I played a game of wandering up and down stairs and hallways without being seen by the servants. Now I slipped into Edward's room without being discovered.

I found a bowl, filled it with warm water, and washed the baby, laughing with pleasure at his squirmy, slippery body. All the while, his dark eyes never left my face. In all the years since Edward's death, Mother had kept everything of his, and so I took one of Edward's undershirts and put it on the baby, making a nightgown. I then struggled with towels and safety pins to make a kind of diaper.

I was sure the baby must be hungry. "I promise I'll be right back," I told him. He looked at me, not crying, not making a sound, as if he had long ago given up having anything to say about what happened to him. I laid him gently on a blanket I had placed on the floor.

First I went to the kitchen, where our cook, Gopel, was sitting smoking a *bidi*. He was leafing through an old copy of *Country Life* magazine of Mother's. He jumped up, but when he saw that it was only me and not Mother or Father, he went back to the cigarette and the magazine. Gopel was a small man, but he was very strong, and I loved to watch him attack coconuts with his knife and break them open with a single blow. When he'd pried out the tender meat, he always gave me a piece to chew. "The British have women in their army," he said. "Look here." He pointed to a photograph of a fox-hunting party of men and women.

"They are only hunting foxes. Like they hunt tigers here. Gopel, I'm hungry. Can I have something from the icebox?"

He started to put the magazine aside. "No, no," I said hastily, "I'll help myself."

He shrugged and went back to turning the pages. The icebox was in a small room out of Gopel's sight. "Don't leave the door open, Missy Sahib," he called. Ice had to be brought by ship and was very precious. I wasn't sure what a baby would eat. I grabbed milk and some porridge, which Gopel made each night to have ready for Father's breakfast.

When I returned to Edward's room, it seemed a miracle that the baby was still there.

At first the porridge was spit out, and I guessed he was used to rice, but after a bit he ate the porridge and commenced to wriggle his arms and legs in the first sign I had that the baby was healthy and had a mind of its own. Thinking of what might have happened to his little legs, I was convinced I had done the right thing, but I wasn't at all sure Mother and Father would think so.

I spent the next hour memorizing the baby: his hair that grew in soft swirls, his brown eyes with their fringe of long lashes, the perfect small fingers and toes. I couldn't understand how it was possible to buy such a thing, and now that I had bought it, I didn't see how I could let it go. I was frantic with possession. I think I would have killed to keep him. I wanted things for him: proper clothes, toys, nourishing food. I wanted to read him stories and teach him my favorite poems. I wanted to show him off and tell everyone that he was mine. I decided he must have a name and thought of how I had found him under the bridge. I named him Nadi, the Hindi word for *river*.

Nadi's little face darkened, and he began to cry. I tried more porridge. I checked the towel, and it didn't need changing. I picked him up and walked with him, cradling him in my arms as I had seen people do with babies. I sang to him. Still he cried. What if he was sick? Nadi was too complicated for me. I knew I couldn't keep him hidden away in the room like a toy I would sometimes play with. So what was I going to do? Just as I was ready to give up, Nadi stopped crying, and a few minutes later, I heard Mother and Father return. I placed Nadi gently on the bed with pillows around him so he wouldn't fall off, and made a dash for my room, throwing myself, with all my clothes on, into my bed and pulling up the cover.

Mother looked into my darkened room, as she always did, to say good night. "It was a lovely party," she said. "When the sun went down, it was cool enough to wander in their gardens. Everything smelled of jasmine, and they have such a clever gardener who manages to grow roses. What did you do this evening?"

"Nothing. I read a little and sat outside and looked at the moon."

"We shouldn't have left you alone, but I have a surprise. Your Father has some business in Calcutta, and he's taking us with him to spend the day. You and I can shop while he's at his meetings."

"Oh, I can't," I said. The minute the words were out of my mouth, I realized what I had done.

"What do you mean, you can't? You're always coaxing to go to Cal."

It was true. I longed to see the famous Indian city I had heard so much about, but I couldn't leave Nadi, not for a day, not even for an hour. "I'm not feeling very well," I said.

"What's wrong? Should I call Dr. Morton?"

"No. It's just my stomach. I had some sherbet at the bazaar."

"Oh, Rosalind, how often must I tell you not to go

there? Your father would be so upset if he knew. You must promise never to go there again. I'm sure you'll be better in the morning. We can't postpone the trip. Father has appointments all set up. I'll get you some cascara, and we'll put you on a diet of arrowroot and milk."

I swallowed the cascara and managed to convince Mother I was sleepy and sent her on her way. Several times during the night, I got up to check on Nadi. Only once did he awaken, but after a bit of milk and new towels he went back to sleep. The servants were all in their homes, except for one of the bearers who slept in the kitchen. No one saw me, but tomorrow the servants would be everywhere. Though they seldom went into Edward's room, they would be able to hear Nadi if he cried.

In the morning, when Mother came into my room, I pushed aside my curtain of mosquito netting and, looking as sad as I could, said that I must stay in bed, that I felt too sick to travel. "Your father will be so disappointed, but clearly you are better off at home if you are ill. I'll call Dr. Morton."

"Oh, I'm sure I'll be better. You don't have to call him."

"Nonsense. Of course I'll call him, and I'm not going. Your father can go without me."

Father came into the room just in time to hear what Mother said. "No, indeed, I won't go without you. I've been looking forward to our trip together, and I won't be disappointed. Rosalind looks fine to me. I suspect it is just some nonsense she has cooked up to get out of going. I suppose you have a young man waiting for you at the club."

It was Father's pretense that I had a number of beaus hanging about and vying for my attention. That there was no evidence of this didn't matter to him.

I played along. "Well, to tell you the truth, there is a someone I was going to meet at the club. Max Nelson." Max Nelson was the only boy whose name I knew.

Mother looked relieved. She said to Father, "I saw Rosalind talking to the Nelson boy at the club yesterday."

"He was in my regiment. A brave fellow, but one to do things his way. Not a quality one wants in a soldier. Still, he's young, and I suspect he'll shape up." Father appeared pleased that his fantasies of my popularity were not so far from the mark. "Well, if you're sure. Your mother has looked forward to this little trip. It's been pretty dull for her during the war. Chance for a little shopping." No more was said about Dr. Morton.

The minute I heard the car pull away for the railway station, I jumped out of bed and hurried down to the kitchen for more milk and porridge, assuring Gopel it was all I wanted and that I was too sick to sit down and eat it. "I'll have it in bed," I said, and fixed myself a tray, which I carried down the back passageway to Nadi.

With Mother and Father gone, I was able to sneak out of my room and spend hours playing with Nadi. I found lots of the baby things of Edward's that Mother had saved, and they fitted Nadi perfectly. I loved dressing him up. When he whimpered, I rocked him in my arms and sang to him all the songs I knew by heart—"For All the Saints," "Rule Britannia," "Till we meet again"—and recited the Jabberwocky poem from *Alice in Wonderland*.

In the early evening he was sleeping soundly, and I thought I ought to go down to dinner so no one would be suspicious. I sat alone at the long dining table and choked down a dinner of mutton and potatoes so that everyone would think I was feeling better and leave me alone. The cook had made me a special white pudding that jiggled as the bearer carried it in. He set it down proudly in front of me. I ate half of it and told the bearer that I would take the rest up to my room to eat later.

With my stomach so full of mutton and potatoes I could barely move, I mounted the back stairway, eager to feed Nadi the pudding. But when I opened the door to Edward's room, I found the room empty.

4

For a moment I was afraid the Cobra had discovered Nadi and carried him off. Then I thought Nadi might have crawled away, but how could he have opened the door? I looked under the bed and behind the furniture and the curtains. I flung the pillows about and turned out the dresser drawers. I looked in the passageway and the nearby rooms. As I came down the stairs I heard a baby's cries. I followed the cries to the hallway, and there was Amina holding Nadi, surrounded by all the servants. Ranjit was there and Gopel, and one of the gardeners. Ranjit was very angry. He was accusing every one of them of breaking into Edward's room and hiding a baby.

For just a moment I thought of keeping silent rather than endure Ranjit's anger. Surely he would tell Mother and Father. But Nadi was mine. I was afraid of what might happen to him if I didn't claim him. "It's the old sweeper's grandchild," I said. "I bought him for a shilling from the Cobra—I mean, Pandy—the man who twists the legs of the little children to make them beggars."

"Oh, oh," Ranjit wailed. "What will your parents say? They will accuse us of letting you wander in dangerous places. And to steal a baby!"

"I didn't steal him; I bought him with my own money. You don't have to tell my parents. I'll find a place for the baby."

Amina said, "It is true what Rosalind tells. Aziz heard that the baby was sold to Pandy."

Ranjit's face was a storm. "The master and mistress must be told and the baby given back to the old sweeper."

I snatched Nadi from Amina, pressing his warmth close to me. "The sweeper will just sell him again. Isn't there anyone among the servants who would keep the baby and take care of it?"

"Missy Sahib," Ranjit said, "I am sorry to say it, but you are a foolish girl. It takes all their wages to care for their own children, and even if they had the money, they would not take into their homes the child of a sweeper."

It was at that moment that I thought of Mrs. Nelson and her orphanage. "I know someone who will take the baby," I said. Of course, I knew nothing of whether she would take him, but it would gain me time. "I'll take him to Memsahib Nelson. I'll go right now."

I could see Ranjit and Amina were anxious to get Nadi out of the house and away from their responsibility. "How do you know this?" Ranjit asked.

"The Memsahib Nelson has an orphanage," I said. "They take children who have no home."

"They would take a baby such as this one? A sweeper's child?" Amina asked.

As convincingly as I could I said, "Yes, I'm sure of it."

Ranjit said, "If your Mother and Father learn that you ventured out and stole a baby, your parents will surely blame me for the bad thing that happened on my watch."

"If you are certain that the orphanage place will take the baby," Amina said, "then we must go there, and at once. Anything that will get the baby out of the house must be a good thing."

Ranjit drew himself up and with all his authority pronounced, "You must take this baby to the Memsahib, but

Amina must go with you. If they do not take it, the baby must go back to the old sweeper."

There was a little booklet with the names, phone numbers, and home addresses of all the British families on the cantonment. I quickly found where the Nelsons lived. Amina insisted on carrying Nadi. "You would walk in public with an Indian baby in your arms? Oh, you have caused so much trouble. I don't know what your mother and father will say. There will be so many words." I bit my tongue to keep from letting Amina know it was her own daughter, Isha, who got me to buy Nadi.

When we came to the Nelson's home, we were taken aback. Of course in the past there had been glimpses through the gates of the walled green lawns, the gaudy peacocks with their tails like a boast and the house that stretched forever, but now we had to walk through the impressive gates and into the elegant grounds with no sounds but the *tick-ticki* of the little lizards and the cry of a night heron. I told the guard at the gate that I wished to see Mrs. Nelson. He looked from the baby to Amina, who, awed by her surroundings and embarrassed at being part of such strange proceedings, had drawn her *sari* over her face. Finally, pointing to Amina and Nadi, he said, "They can wait here. You can go to the house, Missy Sahib."

I took Nadi in my arms and said, "I am a friend of Memsahib Nelson's." Without waiting for his permission, I walked up to the entrance with Amina, who refused to let me out of her sight. Before I could knock, the front door swung open, and there was Max Nelson.

"Hello," he said. "It's Rosalind, isn't it? Whose baby have you?"

"It's mine," I said.

His eyebrows shot up. "You'd better come in." He held the door for me and for Amina, who hurried inside with a haughty glance at the guard. Max led us down a long marble hallway and into a large room. The windows had been shuttered against the last of the sun, and a *punkah* was slowly revolving overhead, giving the room a shadowed coolness. The sofas and chairs were oversize and covered with throws and pillows in bright colors. On one of the tables was a blue Chinese bowl filled with large red amaryllis blooms. A wall of shelves held a library of books. On another wall were small paintings not much larger than pages in a book. When he saw me looking at them, Max led me closer. "Mogul paintings," he said. "This one done more than a hundred years ago."

Gloria Whelan

On the trip, Nadi had been quiet. Now he was awake and squirming. He began to cry. "He needs to eat," I said.

Max gave me a strange look. I blushed and hastily said, "Do you suppose you could get a little milk and porridge or rice? And then I need to see your mother. I want to give her my baby."

"Milk, rice, and Mother. You shall have them all, but are you sure you want to give up your child?"

Amina gasped. "Missy Sahib," she whispered, "tell Sahib Nelson where the baby comes from."

But I was enjoying Max's confusion, so I only teased, "I'll tell you all about it when your mother comes."

In no time a bearer appeared with a tray on which I saw milk and a little bowl of cooked rice. Nadi was happily swallowing the rice when Mrs. Nelson arrived followed by Max. "I understand you wish to give me a baby, and Max says it is yours?"

"Well, not exactly." I told her the whole story, only leaving out Isha's name, for I didn't want to betray Isha to Amina.

Mrs. Nelson said, "Rosalind, how is it you know so much about this Pandy and his evil behavior? Are you so often in the bazaar?"

Before I could answer, Amina said, "Oh, Memsahib, we would never knowingly allow the Missy Sahib to go into the bazaar, but she is a willful girl, and what are we to do?"

Mrs. Nelson exchanged glances with Max and then turned to me. "You are not to worry about the baby, Rosalind. The orphanage is for just such children. We will take him and see that he is well cared for." She held out her arms.

"His name is Nadi," I said. "That means *river* in Hindi." Still I held on to him.

"Then of course we will call him Nadi."

I could not let go of Nadi.

Mrs. Nelson said, "You can visit the orphanage and see Nadi as often as you like."

With that, I had the courage to give Nadi to Mrs. Nelson, but my heart felt as empty as my arms.

Mrs. Nelson made cheerful cooing sounds at the baby, but when she turned to me her look was sober. "You understand, Rosalind that I will have to discuss this with your parents. What they say will make no difference about Nadi—Nadi will be cared for at the orphanage—but your mother and father should be aware of what has happened. You can be sure that I will explain to them that what you did was a loving and unselfish thing. They cannot be angry at how well you meant, but for you to have been wandering about among the thieves under the bridge and dealing with a man like Pandy is troubling."

Max was looking fondly at Nadi. "Mother, just think what a miserable fate that baby would have had if it weren't for Rosalind. She ought to have a medal, not a scolding."

"There is no question of a scolding, Max, but if you were in a dangerous situation, I would want to know about it."

Max smiled fondly at his mother. "Would you have had Major James write to you each time we went into battle?"

"Yes, so I could have prayed even harder. Don't tease me, Max. You know what I mean. I have a responsibility to Rosalind's parents, but you can be sure I will tell them how brave she was and how her courage saved this child. Now you must see Rosalind and Amina to their home. It's getting dark out, and they will need an escort." With that, she leaned across the baby in her arms to kiss my forehead. "Don't forget to visit Nadi," she said.

Amina grumbled all the way home. "Oh, what will Sahib James and Memsahib say? They will blame us."

"No, Amina, it was all my fault. You didn't know

anything about it. I'll take the blame. I deserve it. But I'm not sorry I did it, and I'd do it all over again."

"That's the spirit," Max said. "I don't suppose those two girls you were with at the club would have taken that chance."

I smiled as I thought of Amy dealing with Pandy. "I hope this doesn't get out at the club." I could imagine the withering looks and whispers.

"My lips are sealed, and Mother won't say a word except to your parents. I'm sure your parents won't spread it about." He indicated Amina. "Your servants will be loyal as well."

My parents had returned from Calcutta, and Father was at the door looking for me. "Good evening, Lieutenant Nelson, I had not expected that you would be on a mission like this one."

Max stamped his feet and saluted. "Glad to serve, sir."

"Amina, I think Memsahib would like to see you. Lieutenant, we have just had a call from your mother. It was most kind of her to take an interest in Rosalind's folly. I'm very appreciative of her willingness to care for the child, but embarrassed that we have put her in so awkward a position."

"Not at all, sir. It's what the orphanage is for. Mother will take good care of Rosalind's baby."

Father straightened into full military position and glared at Max, who blanched beneath his tan. Hastily Max added, " Of course, I mean the sweeper's baby."

"Yes, well, thank you so much for seeing my daughter home safely. I won't keep you."

Max did a kind of military turn and walked hastily down the path. Father closed the door very carefully, as if it might fly out of his hands. With a glance at Ranjit, who was hovering nearby, he said, "Rosalind, I want to see you in my study."

A moment later Mother hurried in and threw her arms around me. "Oh, Rosalind, what have you done? And Edward's room! Everything there is turned upside down."

Father hastily closed the door and said, "Cecelia, there is no need for dramatics. Rosalind has been very foolish. I can't think how she became involved in this scandalous matter."

Father was talking as if I weren't there, so I had to speak up. "Father, you wouldn't let the Cobra hurt Nadi like he did the other children?"

"I don't want to hear about the so-called Cobra person.

He has nothing to do with us. Do you think you can forge ahead and solve all of India's problems? That is entirely an Indian matter."

"But you are always saying that we British are here to help India."

"Not in sordid matters like this."

"Harlan," Mother said, "she saved that child from a horrible fate."

"Would you have our daughter wandering about the slums of India by herself every night snatching children from anyone that she felt was not giving them proper care?"

I accused, "If you hadn't fired the sweeper, his family wouldn't have had to sell the baby."

I should never have said that, for Father was livid. "Are you trying to blame me for this misadventure? It was a great mistake for me to give in to your mother and keep you here in India instead of sending you to England long ago when I wanted to. Thank heavens it is not too late. Ships are sailing again."

Mother grabbed at Father's arm. "What are you suggesting? That we send Rosalind to England? That country is far more dangerous than this one. Think what happened to little Edward. At least here we can keep Rosalind safe."

"Do you call letting her wander about in the bazaar and among the huts of thieves keeping her safe!"

Mother began to cry. "I know it is all my fault," she said to Father, "but you were gone and I wasn't well, and it was all too much for me. Now you are back, and it won't happen again."

The threat of being sent away to England had sobered me. Gone was all my passion for saving the children of India. All I cared about was saving myself from being sent away. "I'm so sorry, Father, I'll never go back to the bazaar. I'll spend all my time at the club, really, I will. I promise."

I don't think it was my promise as much as Mother's tears that changed his mind, but after a lot of glowering, Father said, "Very well, but you are not to involve yourself in any way with what goes on in this country. Those who are older and wiser than you are have things well in hand. Is that understood?"

"Yes, Father," I said in my meekest voice.

Mother dried her tears.

5

Mother and I hurried to the club the next day and the day after and the day after that. The town was parched waiting for the monsoon, and little puffs of dust rose wherever you walked, but the club was an oasis of green and blossom. A *chota mali* hurried about with a sprinkling can to water the red poinsettias and pink roses while another scraped the dew off the grass so the hot sun would not burn it. Two men were halfheartedly swatting balls in the bright sun of the tennis court.

Mother played endless rubbers of bridge while I did what was expected of me. I swam in the pool and spent long hours sipping lemonade while Sarah and Amy gossiped or

talked about clothes and how skirts were becoming shorter
and shorter and how with the war over, we'd get the latest
fashions from England. The lemonade was warm, I didn't
know half the people Sarah and Amy gossiped about, the
pool was crowded, and I didn't care about the length of
skirts or the newest fashions. I missed Isha and the excitement of the bazaar.

Always I looked for Max, but he never came. Mrs. Nelson was seldom there, but whenever I saw her I would
hover near her until I could manage to ask quietly how
Nadi was. "He's doing beautifully," Mrs. Nelson always
said. She would add, "You must come and pay him a visit."

"Mother," I pleaded, "let's go and see Nadi, please." At
first Mother refused. "Impossible," she said. I knew she was
afraid of what Father would think. He had forbidden any
mention of Nadi.

"Water under the bridge," he insisted. "The sooner the
whole miserable episode is forgotten, the better." Father
was kind to me, but I felt I had stepped over some uncross-
able line. He was on one side, and I was on the other.
He no longer called me Rosy. I was Rosalind now, and it
broke my heart.

Still, I kept pleading with Mother, giving her no peace

until finally she said yes. I think it was because she remembered how it was to be separated from a child. Although my missing Nadi was nothing like her missing Edward, still, she understood my longing.

We chose a day when we were sure Father would be confined to his office with meetings and we could slip through the streets without his seeing us. The orphanage was on the outskirts of the town, so we had to take a bicycle *tonga* through the busy streets. The *tonga wallah* was an old man, and thin. His bones stuck out of his *dhoti,* and twice he had to stop to catch his breath. I tried to conjure up a thinner me, as if by some fantasy I could shed some of the weight he had to bear. Still, in my impatience I urged, *"Chalo, chalo,"* faster, faster.

We made our way through the crowds of the bazaar, and I looked with longing at the stalls where Isha and I did our wishful shopping. We had a near accident as a roaming cow swerved out of the way of an oxcart and into our path, and there were wrong turns, but at last, on the outskirts of the town, we drew up to a large *godown,* a kind of warehouse. There was a row of simal trees, whose blossoms made the trees' branches, bare of leaves, look like they had been doused with buckets of scarlet paint.

A green parakeet hopped from branch to branch. Beyond the warehouse were stretches of gold mustard fields and huddles of small villages.

Mrs. Nelson welcomed us. She explained, "This building was used by my husband to store jute at one time, but now we ship it from closer to the source." Large rooms were sectioned off to accommodate the children's different ages. The older children were gathered into a classroom. There must have been a dozen sitting at desks. In one gesture all their heads turned to stare at us, and then, at a word from their teacher, turned back to their lessons.

"When they come here, most of these children have never been to school," Mrs. Nelson said, "so they are in class year-round to catch up, but this time of year, when it's so hot, there are classes only in the morning."

In another room, three- and four-year-olds were playing a circle game accompanied by a lot of giggling as the teacher tried to get them all to go in the same direction. Mrs. Nelson paused to tell us the stories of a few of the children, but she could see how impatient I was and finally led us to the nursery, where there were several cribs. Two of the babies were only weeks old, but the rest were closer to Nadi's age, three or four months. It was lunchtime for them, and young Indian women dressed in white *saris* held the children on their laps and spooned rice into mouths that eagerly opened like the beaks of baby birds.

For a moment I was unsure, but then I recognized the soft swirls of hair and long lashes. I asked if I could feed Nadi and slipped onto the chair in place of the little Indian *ayah*. Nadi snuggled down into my lap. I grinned like a fool and spooned the rice porridge into his mouth while Mrs. Nelson and Mother looked on. Mrs. Nelson appeared amused, but Mother, thinking of another child, had tears in her eyes. When Nadi had had his fill and began spitting out what I put in, I reluctantly handed him back to his *ayah* and followed Mother and Mrs. Nelson out of the room.

Mrs. Nelson was guiding us to the kitchen, which was to be the last stop on our tour, when Max appeared. He greeted my mother and said to Mrs. Nelson, "If you'll excuse Rosalind from viewing the finer points of the children's diets, I'd like a word with her."

Mother looked puzzled, but Mrs. Nelson merely waved her hand in the air in a kind of dismissal of Max and me. As Mrs. Nelson shepherded mother into the kitchen she was explaining, "Since we have Muslim children as well as

Hindu youngsters, different foods must be prepared—and prepared by different servants, for as you know, Hindus and Muslims cannot touch one another's food."

Max led me to a small office with nothing more than a desk on which papers were heaped as if someone were playing a game to see at what point everything would tumble over. "Mother's too busy to be organized," Max said. "She told me you were coming today." He hesitated, running his fingers through his brown hair so that it stood up like a hedgehog's quills. "You said if ever Gandhi came here to speak, you would like to hear him. Did you mean that?"

"Yes, of course, but my parents would never let me."

"He's going to be talking tomorrow afternoon on the *maidan.*"

The *maidan* was a large parade ground in the middle of the town where military parades, riding competitions, and cricket matches were held. In the rainy season it was a sea of green grass where you might see a goat grazing; this time of year the grass was scorched brown. "How would I get there?"

"Just go to the club as you usually do. Then slip away. The *maidan* is only a short walk, and I'll be at the club to go with you." He gave me a challenging look.

I knew I should say no, but I didn't want Max to think me a coward. At that moment his opinion of me was more important than Father's. Besides, Max was there and Father was somewhere else, and Father need never know. I'd slip out of the club and back again. I was sure none of my parents' friends would be there to hear Gandhi. Of course I wanted to see the famous leader, but I was more excited about being with Max and by the danger of the adventure. All those days of boredom at the club made me hunger to do something rash and daring. "All right," I said. "I'll tell the other girls I'm going into the clubhouse with Mother for a while to watch the bridge game. Mother will think I'm with the girls."

I was wild with anticipation and hardly slept. At breakfast Mother said, "Rosalind, you look feverish. Perhaps you're getting too much sun. Let's stay home today. I don't think I can stand one more day of bridge. It's impossible to concentrate on cards in the heat. Even the club is getting uncomfortable."

"Oh, no. I have to go today. I promised Amy and Sarah."

"I thought those girls bored you."

"Well, yes, they do, but Amy promised to bring a magazine her mother just got from England with all the new fashions."

Mother didn't sound convinced. "I've never known you to take a great interest in the latest fashions."

"Well, you're always telling me I ought to give more thought to my appearance."

Mother sighed. "Very well, we'll go, but after this I want a few days at home to see to the garden and catch up with my letters. Your aunts will think I've disappeared from the face of the earth."

We got to the club in time for tiffin. It was the same boring macaroni and cheese and fruit salad. After lunch, the women got out their cards and I went out to the pool with Amy and Sarah, who headed for the changing room.

When I stayed behind, Amy said, "Aren't you getting into your bathing suit?"

"I don't feel like swimming today," I said. Amy shrugged.

I was to meet Max at three o'clock, so I had an hour to get through. I don't remember anything that was said. It seemed to have nothing to do with me. It was as if Amy and Sarah were birds chirping or horses neighing. I sat there rehearsing my excuse in my head, and all the while I longed to shock Sarah and Amy by telling them what I planned to do. *I'm going into the village,* I'd say, *to a big rally of Indian people to support the Congress Party, and I'm going to hear Mr. Gandhi talk about driving out the British.* Instead I had to keep my secret to myself.

"You're really boring today," Amy said to me. "More than usual."

"I'm sorry. I was thinking about something else." I glanced at my watch. It was nearly three. "I think I'll go in and watch the bridge game for a while. I might take bridge up."

Sarah groaned. "Then you would really be boring."

I headed for the clubhouse, then just inside the door I turned and hurried down a long hallway to the entrance, my heels making a staccato on the tile that I thought everyone would hear and wonder about.

At first I didn't see Max, but then there he was signaling to me. We left the club and joined the surge of people, nearly all Indian, pushing their way through the street toward the *maidan.* As we wedged our way into the stream the crowd all but swept us off our feet. Max hung on to me. When I looked up, I saw an expression of glee on his face, as if he were a child who had gotten away with mischief. My own excitement died when I saw uniformed Indian police and British soldiers take positions around the *maidan*. Max noticed as well. He drew me deeper into the crush of the crowd so we wouldn't be as visible, for there were only a handful of non-Indians.

"Don't worry about the police," he said. "They're just here to intimidate people. Gandhi has a perfect right to speak."

There were cries of "Gandhiji, Gandhiji," which meant the honorable Gandhi. Max hung on to me. The crowd was like a wild river, and its current washed us to the front, directly under a box that had been set up for the speakers. A man was introducing Gandhi, praising him and calling him the man who would free India from Britain and referring to him as Mahatma.

"That means 'great soul,'" Max whispered. "Britain has had its hands on India for three hundred years. Queen Victoria called India the star in her crown. While Canada and Australia have already wrestled free from Britain's control, the Indian people are not allowed to rule their own land. I honestly believe and hope that before I have finished studying history at Cambridge, English history will have changed and Gandhi will have changed it."

Finally, Gandhi himself stood upon the box. I was dis-appointed, for he was only a small man in a white *dhoti*. He peered out at us through round eyeglasses as if we were a book he was considering reading. After quite a long moment of silence during which the crowed stilled as if he had cast a spell over them, Gandhi began to speak.

He said the Indian people must never go to war with the British over their desire for independence, but instead use only nonviolence. "We must conserve our anger and turn it into energy to accomplish our goal. I don't want India to practice nonviolence because she is weak. I want her to practice nonviolence being conscious of her strength and power."

At first the audience was quiet, as if they were disap-pointed at being told to give up the idea of fighting, but then Gandhi said, "Nonviolence is a weapon of the brave. It is the greatest force at the disposal of mankind." At that there was a great cheer.

At that moment the police and the soldiers began to close in on the crowd, ordering us to disperse. The man who had introduced Gandhi now tried to spirit him off. Gandhi refused to leave, standing upon the box and continuing to talk, but there was so much confusion that you could no longer hear what he said. People rushed here and there, trying to get away. We remembered the massacre at Amritsar, and we were all afraid that we, too, would be fired upon.

There was no firing upon the crowd, but the police were pushing people away from the *maidan,* and a few of the police were wielding *lathis.* I hung on to Max, who was trying to get us through the fleeing crowd when a senior British police officer noticed us. "Just a minute, there." He looked at us like someone who has discovered valuable coins lying in the street. "What are you two doing here? Do you know you are involving yourselves in treason? You had better come with me."

The word *treason* terrified me. I knew what they did with traitors. They shot them at sunrise.

Max tried to explain. "We were just curious, sir. We saw the crowd and thought we'd find out what was going on."

"And when you found out, you stayed on to hear what that troublemaker had to say. You should have known better, and you certainly ought not to have allowed this young lady to be here."

As he marched us off I looked back at Gandhi, who

was being led away by a policeman, a look of peace on his face, as if he were going on a pleasant visit. While several of the crowd were placed in a wagon and driven off, we were placed in a police car, Max in front and me in back, so there was no chance to talk together. At the police station we were again separated. Max was led away, having only a second to give me an apologetic look, and I was ushered into a small room containing a table and two chairs. The officer who had arrested us followed me in and, after telling me to sit down, took the chair across the table.

"Now, young lady," he said, "just who are you?" He said it kindly, and I began to feel there would be no shooting at sunrise.

"Rosalind James."

"James? You wouldn't be any relation to Major Harlan James?"

"Yes, sir. I'm his daughter."

The policeman stared at me. "I daresay your father will be a little surprised to learn of your adventure. Since I know him, I'll just have an officer drop you off at your home, but I don't want to see you at one of these revolutionary get-togethers again. Is that understood?"

6

Ranjit answered the door, and on seeing the police officer with me threw up his arms and hurried off to summon Father, who arrived in seconds with Mother shadowing him. The four of us made a little parade into Father's study, where the officer explained why he was escorting me home. One look at Father's face let me know the shooting at sunrise was coming. In a voice like pistol shots Father thanked the officer and dismissed him, but not before saying, "As his commanding officer, I will deal with Lieutenant Nelson. You may tell him so."

Father's voice was like steel. "Your mother informed

me she went to look for you at the club and you had disappeared."

Mother hastily said, "I didn't say 'disappeared,' dear, I only said I wasn't able to find Rosalind. I thought perhaps she wasn't feeling well and had gone home by herself so as not to worry me." Mother gave me a disappointed look, and that was worse than Father's red and angry face.

"I'm sorry," I said.

Father demanded, "Do you have any idea who this man is at whose feet you worshipped today?"

Mother said, "Surely Rosalind was not worshipping at the man's feet, Harlan."

"Indeed she was, and perhaps, Cecelia, you had best leave this to me."

"Yes, Harlan." Mother sank into a chair.

Father turned his attention back to me. "That Gandhi person is an agitator, a revolutionary who would have the people of this country up in arms against the British."

"But, Father, Gandhi is against violence. I heard him say so."

"It doesn't matter what foolishness he is prattling on about. The men who hear him will take matters into their own hands. There will be lawlessness. There will be rebellion and rioting and bloodshed. With your presence there you were condoning it. No, not just condoning it, but sanctioning it."

I had no idea that listening to a harmless man talk about Indian independence from England could have such terrible consequences. "What is so bad about India wanting to rule its own country?"

"You are a fifteen-year-old girl! How can you presume to ask such a question?"

"I only want to know." And I did.

"Indians are children. They aren't ready for self-rule any more than you are."

"Ranjit isn't a child. You said yourself that we couldn't get along without him."

Father turned to Mother. "I cannot believe we have raised so willful and ignorant a child. I take full responsibility. I should have sent Rosalind to England. Instead I gave in to your wishes. These last years with me away have been too much for you, Cecelia. There has been no one here to assume responsibly for this child's education. I only pray it's not too late."

Mother saw where this was leading. "Oh, Harlan,"

she said in almost a whisper, "you can't be thinking of sending Rosalind to England."

"Indeed I am, and the sooner the better. I should have sent her off when she stole that baby and—"

"I didn't steal him. I bought him. And, Father, you should see Nadi now. He is doing so well."

"Harlan," Mother said, "just think about the terrible fate from which Rosalind saved that child. And it's true. Nadi is flourishing."

"You mean, you have allowed Rosalind to continue her association with that child when I have expressly forbidden it? Cecelia, what were you thinking? It is perfectly clear to me that I cannot depend on your good judgment. In my position I will have to travel, and I will not feel comfortable leaving Rosalind in your hands. She's going to your sisters in England, and that's all there is to it."

Mother and I had set our own trap, and now we had fallen into it. We had admitted seeing Nadi, and this was our punishment.

Father sat and rustled some papers on his desk. "I have the sailing schedule here somewhere. I believe there is a steamship leaving in two weeks for England. She can take the train to Bombay from Calcutta." As if he had been rummaging through some revolting dish and found a tasty morsel, Father's expression brightened, and he said, "At last you will have an opportunity to see Cal, Rosalind, something you have been wishing for. And I will see to it that when you get to England, you shall have the best education that money can buy."

And then, as if he thought the enormity of my sin made it unsuitable to finish the scolding on a happy note, Father said, "As to Max Nelson, you are not to see or get in touch with that young man. It is bad enough that a member of the British Armed Forces attended such an outrageous event, but to involve a helpless girl in the affair is unforgivable. I'll see to him myself."

With that, I was sent to my room, the plaintive sound of Mother's sad entreaties, like the coo of mourning doves, following me. Father made only one concession. Since he had to remain in town to greet someone important from England who was traveling to our area on business, Mother would be allowed to accompany me to Calcutta.

7

Preparations began at once. Telegrams were sent to my aunts and return telegrams duly received from them saying they would be delighted to have me. Aunt Louise wrote, "This is wonderful news. We will be so pleased to have dear Rosy with us. Tell her how anxious I am to show her all the wonders of London. I know from her letters that she is a bright and curious child and will enjoy the sights of this great city. I know, too, that she will bring a bit of sunshine into our rather gray years."

Aunt Ethyl's letter was very different. "I can promise you," she wrote to Mother and Father, "that you can rely on me to uphold the high standards of behavior I am sure you have instilled in Rosalind. I do not believe in spoiling young people but feel it is never too soon to instill in them responsibility and duty."

Father was reassured by Aunt Ethyl's words and troubled by Aunt Louise's.

"Louise was always a little light-minded," Father said.

Mother took me aside to tell me that I might notice little disagreements between her sisters. "I'm afraid they are like chalk and cheese. Louise is the optimist and Ethyl the one to look for the next disaster. Ethyl has always been a bit stiffnecked. She is our older sister, and when my parents died quite young it fell to her to watch over us. I must say she kept a very firm hand on us. I had the greatest difficulty getting her to let me marry your father, and she was upset when I said I was going off to India. In fact, she refused to speak to me for weeks, and there was some other unpleasantness, but Louise was not so lucky as I was."

Even in my misery about having to leave, I was curious about what I was going to and intrigued at learning that there might be mystery and drama in my future. "What do you mean?" I asked.

"Perhaps I shouldn't tell you all of this, but it will help you understand your aunts. Of course, you must never mention a word of the story. Shortly after I left for India, Louise fell in love and wanted to marry. I believe they had even engaged St. Margaret's Church for the wedding. I never had a chance to meet the young man, so I couldn't say what really happened, but Ethyl put an end to it. I always felt guilty, believing that Ethyl wished to keep one of us with her and that my going off meant Louise would have difficulty escaping. But I shouldn't be telling tales. Ethyl has a great many good qualities. She can't be blamed for taking her responsibility to look after Louise and me too seriously. And she is so dependable, your father and I will have no worries on your account. Certainly there will be no spoiling you. Ethyl knows the value of a shilling."

Apart from a few cotton dresses, there were not many clothes to pack, because I had nothing suitable for the cold weather ahead of me. Instead, Father would send money for my aunts to outfit me. There were some things I insisted on packing. I had a paisley shawl of such soft wool you could pass the entire shawl through a ring. And there was a pair of handsome silver earrings I had bought in the bazaar with my shilling from two Christmases ago. I had never been able to wear them, because Mother wouldn't let me pierce my ears, but I loved to hold them up to my ears to see how fine they looked. Mother added pictures of Father and of her and a little box of lovely notepaper decorated with roses, for my letters home.

I wandered through our house and our garden memorizing everything so my impressions of them would last in the years I would be in England. "Until you have finished your schooling," Mother said. There was no question of university, for Father had pronounced, "Girls don't need to clutter their minds," so I would be home in three years, one thousand ninety-five days.

When Father was away at the office and Mother in town shopping for underwear for me, something I had no desire to help with, I sneaked away in search of Isha, who was sorry to see me leave but could talk of only one thing. "I am going to have a baby," she confided. "Every morning when my *sass,* Aziz's mother, makes her *puja,* she asks Shiva to give her a grandson. She is much nicer to me now. I am not to lift anything heavy, and she even sweeps the courtyard herself."

I told her how pleased for her I was, and for a moment I wished I could have Nadi back, but then I thought of all the work of caring for a baby and how that would take over Isha's life, so that there would be no more trips to the bazaar.

I begged to see Nadi before I left, but Father would
not have it, and I didn't want to make him angry with
Mother. Ever since Father announced he was sending me
to England, she spent more time on the chaise longue. It
was the hottest time of the year, and there were dust storms.
The pink blossoms hung listlessly on the acacia trees. Even
the bright feathers of the parakeets faded. Mother's heart
problems were always at the back of my mind. She never
mentioned her health to Father, who considered days
when she had to rest a kind of weakness of character on
Mother's part. I worried about her going to Calcutta with
me, yet I wanted her with me and would not give up even
a day that we might be together.

I tried to find out from Father what had happened to
Max. "I hope he isn't in trouble," I said. "He isn't a revolutionary at all. He's studying history at Cambridge and just
wanted to hear what Gandhi was saying. If you are studying history, don't you have to know such things?"

"There is a great difference between studying dangerous doctrines and falling victim to them. Anyhow, we need
not concern ourselves with the young man. He is no longer in India but on his way back to Cambridge. I believe
we will hear nothing more from him."

It made me feel a little better about being sent to England, knowing Max would be there.

We left on a sweltering day when the air was so hot and the birds still rested in the trees instead of flying about, and even little winged insects swooned, falling to the ground. The monsoon rains were overdue, and we kept looking at the sky, hoping the white puffs would turn into storm clouds. All the British were wearing their *topees*. It was my first train trip, and for a moment the excitement of the station—luggage *wallas, chai wallahs* offering cups of tea, and hawkers running up and down the platform selling fresh fruit and delicious-looking *samosas* and *puris*—made me forget how much I hated leaving. But when the train pulled out and the figure of Father standing wistfully by the tracks grew smaller and smaller and then disappeared altogether, I reached over and took Mother's hand and hung on, afraid that she would vanish as well. The trip to Calcutta was only a half-day, but with the train windows open cinders flew into our compartment, and with the windows closed it was so hot you had to fight for every breath. The conductor took one look at Mother and sent a porter with a bowl of ice and a cloth so she could cool her forehead.

The enormous Howrah train station in Calcutta was like a series of villages with families huddled around their belongings. Some were stretched out asleep; others had built small fires and were cooking meals. Children ran about and had to be called back by frantic mothers. Vendors moved about the families hawking roasted chickpeas and puffed rice. One woman had lit a candle at a tiny shrine and was making her *puja*.

Following behind the cart of our luggage *wallah,* we made our way through the station and out into the streets. Thankfully the monsoon, with its promise of relief from the heat, arrived the very moment we reached Calcutta. There were claps of thunder and then waterfalls of rain. Children danced in the streets in thankfulness, their wet clothes clinging to them like second skins. Mother put up her umbrella to shelter us, and we had our luggage loaded onto a cart to go to the hotel while we followed in a horse *tonga,* for cars were sinking into the muddy ruts and stalling. The street was like a river, with people scurrying about under black umbrellas like so many beetles. Men held their shoes in their hands to protect them from the deep water. The horse that drew our *tonga* could barely lift its hooves out of the mud. In a horse *tonga* you faced away from the horses and from the direction you were heading in, so my first view of Calcutta was all backward. I seemed to be leaving it even before I got there.

It rained all afternoon and evening, and after a light supper, mother rested in her room while I got used to the novelty of living somewhere besides my own home. Everything in the hotel bedroom was interesting because it was strange to me. Instead of my usual washbowl and pitcher of water, there was a basin right in my room with faucets that allowed me to turn on hot or cold water whenever I liked. The dresser was covered with a scarf embroidered with bouquets of forget-me-nots, and in one of the drawers I found part of a candy bar left behind by the last person to occupy the room, which set me to wondering who the mysterious person was and thinking perhaps it was Max on his way to England and Cambridge. I fell asleep to the noises on the street and the chirping of Calcutta crickets.

By the next morning the rains had cooled the city. Mother ordered an early breakfast, which we had in our rooms—a wonderful luxury—and then we hurried out to see the city before the next shower arrived. Our *tonga* took us down Chowringhee, Calcutta's main street. We came at once to Calcutta's *maidan,* a park of many acres set on the Hugli River with its swamps and its *ghats* leading down to the water. Along the banks of the river was the two-hundred-year-old Fort William, its cannons still trained on the city. The fort was ringed round with a moat and guarded by as many soldiers as pins in a pincushion. Father had told me the fort was the headquarters of the Eastern Command of the Indian Army and could hold ten thousand soldiers all at once. He said Indian rebels had once been tied to the mouth of the cannons and blown to bits. I tried to imagine that little man, Gandhi, standing alone and, looking out at the great stone pile, calling out that he wanted the British out of India and thinking he would be successful without resorting to violence.

At the far end of the *maidan* a great white marble palace shone in the sun. "The Victoria Memorial," Mother said. "Built to honor the queen." It wasn't quite finished, and there was scaffolding still on one side, but we climbed down from the *tonga* and wandered about with the other tourists. There were many Indians admiring the memorial, which seemed strange to me, for why would they want a big building dedicated to the queen who had ruled over them instead of giving them their freedom. Mother smiled and said, "Perhaps there have been times recently when you have not been happy to suffer your father's authority, but I hope you still respect him."

The streets of Calcutta were so crowded, the *tonga* could barely move about. It was our town multiplied by a thousand. We passed large mansions surrounded by walls and streets of shacks built one next to the other with laundry fluttering in the light breeze, yards and yards of brightly colored *saris*. We passed the buildings of the High Court, on whose roof two storks nested. At Dalhousie Square we saw the General Post Office and, in the distance, St. Paul's Cathedral. We wandered through the enormous galleries of the Indian Museum, where we found gold jewels and elephant skeletons displayed side by side.

Our last stop was the Park Street Cemetery. There were angels with sheltering wings, pyramids, and the small marble houses that were mausoleums. It was so crowded, there was room for only a few shaggy palm trees and small areas of grass. We could barely make our way between the rows of headstones with inscriptions of British children who had died in India of some childhood disease. When years later the families left to go back to England, they had to leave their child behind to lie in an untended grave.

One inscription read, WE LEAVE INDIA, BUT OUR HEARTS REMAIN HERE WITH OUR BELOVED SON.

"How sad," Mother said. I knew she was thinking of my brother lying so far from her in England, an England she had not seen since she left it as a bride.

"Mother, when I get to England, I'll be sure to visit Edward's grave."

"Yes, do that, dear. The summer will be nearly over, but if you could find some daisies . . . When he was little, we would play 'I love you, I love you not' with the flowers, and he would always make 'I love you' come out right. 'I do love you, Mother,' he would say, 'so it's all right if I cheat a bit.'"

After our visit to the cemetery, Mother was very quiet. At the hotel she sent me on to have dinner alone in the dining room, saying she was going to rest. Seeing her pale face and remembering her sadness in the cemetery and her worry about my going to England, I pleaded, "Mother, let's forget about my sailing. Let's go home and tell Father we changed our minds."

"Oh, Rosalind, if only we could. But to face your father's anger would put an end to me."

I wanted Mother to stand up to Father so I would

not have to leave India, but I had learned that Mother did not have the strength. I resolved that if someday such a moment came to me, I would try to be stronger. I went alone to the dining room, but I might as well have stayed in my room, for I had no appetite and every bit of food I put into my mouth was bitter to me.

8

The next morning I met the woman who would
be traveling with me on the train to Bombay and then on
the ship that would take us to England. It seemed odd that
I was to see my own native land for the first time.

"I'm entrusting Rosalind to you," Mother said as she
introduced me to Mrs. Blodget in the lobby of the hotel.
The woman was to join us for breakfast.

"I am sensible of my great responsibility, Mrs. James."

Mother had told me that Mrs. Blodget, along with her
husband, had lived in India for years, sent by a charitable
organization in England to do good deeds. Her husband
had died, and now she wished to return home but lacked

the means. When Mother and Father were looking for someone to accompany me on the trip, Mrs. Blodget had been recommended. In exchange for her chaperoning me, my parents would pay for her travel.

Mrs. Blodget was a small, tidy woman in a simple gray dress with white collar and cuffs. When we were seated at the breakfast table in the hotel dining room, she looked about, an expression of awe on her face. Her order to the waiter was sparse: one boiled egg, toast, and tea. Mother urged her to have sausages or bacon or some of the hotel's famous scones, but Mrs. Blodget shook her head. "I couldn't, Mrs. James. In this country where so many are starving, I feel guilty for every bite I put into my mouth."

Mother looked troubled. "I hope you won't begrudge Rosalind her dinners?"

"Oh, heavens no. It's a pleasure for me to see others enjoying their food. It's only my own conduct that I must account for to William."

"William?" Mother inquired.

"My late husband, William Blodget. He had the highest standards, and I feel him even now looking about at all this luxury with a troubled eye."

The scones Mother and I had spread thickly with marmalade stuck in our throats.

We were to board the Bombay Mail for the journey to our steamer. At the train station I clung to Mother, and we both cried. Mrs. Blodget, watching us, began to cry herself. She assured Mother earnestly, "I promise you, Mrs. James, that I will care for Rosalind like my own child."

Mrs. Blodget headed for the third-class car, but Mother stopped her. "No, no, Mrs. Blodget, look at your tickets. You and Rosalind will be in the first-class sleeper car. You wouldn't want to sit up for forty hours?"

"Oh, I assure you I have traveled all over India in third class. You could feed a dozen families for a year on the difference between first and third class."

"Yes, I'm sure," Mother said, "but as this is Rosalind's first journey to England, we wish it to be a pleasant one. And since you are accompanying her, you must endure first class as well."

The train engine came alive, and puffs of steam exploded into the air. After a final hug, Mother and I separated and I boarded the train. Our compartment had comfortable benches that would turn into beds for the overnight journey and a wide window with little green curtains. I pushed open the window, the better to see Mother, who stood on the platform waving to us, tears streaming down her face. The train picked up speed, and she was gone.

Mrs. Blodget saw my own tears and reached out to take my hand. "My dear, you never leave someone you love. They come right along with you. At this moment William is sitting next to me, and your mother will be as close. You have only to think of her, and she will be here."

Mother's presence was a comforting thought, but I was not so sure how I felt about William being there. And he was. He went with us to the dining car as well. Mrs. Blodget surprised me by ordering generously from the menu, but her choices were strange: not much in the way of soup and meat, but much bread and rice, more than I would have thought she could possibly swallow.

"William has given me an idea," she said, looking positively gleeful. She took a few bites of this and that and then gathered the remaining food into a napkin. "You take your time, my dear, and enjoy what looks like a delightful meal, and I'll just take this into the third-class cars. I know from experience there will be Indian families traveling who will not have a crumb to last them the long journey." She deftly removed a bit of bread from my plate and tucked it into her napkin.

She ignored the beady eye of the waiter and scurried through the dining car in the direction of third class, leaving me with a large plate of roast beef and so guilty a conscience I could not swallow it.

When we were both together again in our compartment, I asked how things had gone. "Oh, they were most thankful," she said. "I promised I would come again after our breakfast. There was a woman there about to have a baby, and I tried to get the conductor to exchange her ticket with mine so that the poor thing could have the privacy of our compartment to give birth, but the cruel-hearted man refused."

I tried to imagine a baby being born right in front of me and how I would cut an umbilical cord without scissors. "Is William here now?" I asked, wondering what he would think of next.

"Not just now, my dear. He comes and goes. He is there when he is needed, but he never intrudes. He was like that when he was alive. If he peeked in and saw I was busy with some needlework or deep into a favorite book, he would leave me at my leisure, but when there was a need to be met he would not leave me alone until the task was accomplished."

Before climbing in to the beds the porter had fashioned for us from our benches, we each said our prayers. I suspect in Mrs. Blodget's prayers the whole world went first class. In my prayers I begged for Mother's health and Nadi's happiness and Father's forgiveness and for Mr. Gandhi, that he would be successful without making the British too angry.

We went directly from the train to the steamer. The train had been one thing—I was still on Indian soil—but the moment I stepped onto the ship for our journey of three weeks, I knew I was leaving India behind. Mrs. Blodgett felt it too, for before she followed me up the gangplank, she reached down and gathered a handful of dirt. "I must take something of India with me," she said.

The steward who settled in our luggage announced that our cabin was on the starboard side. "Always sail on the port side on your outward bound journey. You want the starboard on the return," he said. I wondered how I would endure three years of waiting for the return journey, but a glance at Mrs. Blodgett's forlorn face made me grateful that I, at least, would be coming back.

I began to worry when I saw how comfortable our stateroom was, with its white paneled walls and its porthole looking out on the ocean, its two beds, two comfortable chairs, and even a little dresser, but Mrs. Blodget made no complaints. Instead she appeared to take pleasure in fingering the satin spreads with the liner's initials and exploring the ingenious washing basin and toilet facilities. Perhaps William was allowing her some little pleasure, or perhaps he was busy elsewhere.

At once we made ourselves at home and began to unpack. Mother had bought me two silk dresses to wear for dinner. Mrs. Blodget also unpacked two dresses, but they appeared to be identical to the simple gray one she had on. Our meals were taken in a handsome dining room where the tables were dressed with white linen cloths and little silver vases with fresh flowers. The waiters were friendly but correct, though a little disappointed when Mrs. Blodget refused the champagne the first night out. "Oh my, no!" she said when it was offered, and I could feel William nodding his head in fervent agreement.

We had been assigned to a table for six. The other

passengers were a Mr. and Mrs. Cammeron and a Mr. and Mrs. Dristant. Both couples were returning to England for leaves of absence after long stays in India. Mr. Cammeron had something to do with the Indian trains and Mr. Dristant with the Indian civil service. They would be returning to India in a few months, so they didn't share either Mrs. Blodget's or my sorrow in leaving; on the contrary, the women talked of nothing but the pleasures of London and how they would be shopping at Liberty of London and Harrods. The men spoke of cricket matches and lunches at their club. "How refreshing it will be to return to civilization," Mrs. Cammeron said, causing Mrs. Blodget to say, "It is civilization you will be leaving. The Indians were building great cities when the British were still in animal skins."

At that, there was silence at our table, and ever afterward the Cammerons and the Dristants talked only among themselves, confining their conversation with us to asking for the salt to be passed or inquiring politely if we had had a pleasant day.

Our days were pleasant enough. Mrs. Blodget led me on brisk walks around the deck, went with me to the library, keeping an eye on my choices, and accompanied me to church service on Sundays. In the evenings she screened the movies that were shown for "suitable" ones. Yet all the care in the world could not keep me from spending long hours standing at the railing of the ship, gazing at the sea as it spooled out carrying me farther and farther from India. I never thought of what I was going to, only what I had left. It was all backward and no forward.

There were no empty hours of staring out at the sea for Mrs. Blodget, whom William must have been after again, for the novelty of our pleasant cabin had worn off and she now spent every spare moment in third class, or what she called steerage. She was often up and down the stairway that led to the lower deck, returning with stories of life there. They did not have the food that we did; but, then, most of the passengers were Hindus and would not have eaten the steaks and chops that we were served. Rice was plentiful, Mrs. Blodget said, so there was no need for her to carry food on her trips, "But you can hardly move about," she said, "for the crowding is shameful. That cannot be healthful."

How unhealthful, she soon discovered. One afternoon upon returning to our cabin, I found her scrubbing her hands with great force. "Oh, Rosalind, you cannot imagine the tragedy of it. There is a cholera epidemic below. Only a dozen people so far, but I know from experience how the disease grows in crowded conditions. I have seen whole villages wiped out. William has told me what I already knew: that my place is in steerage, where I am needed. I will take my meals there and get what rest I can when I am not nursing the sick. You are not to get near me, for cholera is highly contagious, and that is another reason for my staying below. I know I can trust you, Rosalind, to behave just as your parents would wish while I am away. One thing more. Do not under any condition say a word about cholera. There would be panic among the passengers if it were known."

With that, Mrs. Blodget took herself off.

I went to the dining room only out of habit, for the report of the deadly disease below decks was so much on my mind that the thought of sitting down to a meal with the chilly Cammerons and Dristants seemed impossible. My table companions looked relieved to find that Mrs. Blodget would not be with us and at once were more kindly toward me.

Mrs. Cammeron said, "I hope your governess is not ill."

"She's not my governess," I said, "just a friend. She did feel a little troubled."

"You must be looking forward to setting foot in England," Mr. Dristant said.

"No, I'm not," I told him, after which I was left alone to worry about what was going on in steerage.

I tried walking laps around the deck. I tried staring out at the sea. I knew it was full of fish and things, but nothing was visible. The surface was a blank, like much of my life was becoming. I knew nothing of the people I had been sitting with. I was on my way to live with strangers, for what did I know of my aunts? I couldn't get hold of my life; it rolled on like the sea, with everything I needed to know hidden away from me. I had never been so alone.

In desperate need of a friendly face, I pushed away the thought of how contagious the cholera might be and decided to go down to steerage to look for Mrs. Blodget. Perhaps I might even be of help. The main stairways were gated, but I found a small spiral stairway hidden away beside a row of lifeboats and climbed down and down until I reached the third class. A row of small cabins lined a long passageway. As I hurried down the corridor I had glimpses through open doors of families huddled into cramped spaces. In some of the staterooms people lay stretched out three to four on narrow cots, moaning. The sight of their misery made me feel like a Peeping Tom, and I kept my eyes to myself.

At the end of the passageway I came upon a large area that must have been the dining room but was now transformed into a hospital. It was crowded with sick people lying on cots and tended by a couple of nurses wearing gauze masks strapped over their faces. Mrs. Blodget was with them. The odor from the results of the illness was so strong I could barely breathe. Skeleton-like hands reached out to grab at my skirt as the people begged for water. There were men and women and small children lying on cots with rumpled and soiled sheets.

Mrs. Blodget rushed over to me. Her words coming through the mask were muffled. "Rosalind! Whatever are you doing here! You mustn't expose yourself to the cholera. You must leave at once before you are seen." She grabbed my arm and with a great yank pulled me after her and out of the sight of the nurses. "How did you get down here? The stairways are sealed off."

"I came down a little stair near the lifeboats."

"Then you must return that way at once."

"But what about you?"

"William has told me I must stay, and even if I should

not want to, I have been so exposed to the disease I would be a terrible menace to anyone who came near me." As if to prove her point, she retreated from me. "Quickly now. I have to get back to the poor patients. We have already had several deaths. When you reach your cabin, you must wash thoroughly." She gave me a strong push down the passageway and left me. I began to run. When at last, out of breath, I reached the stairway, I found a ship's officer fastening a steel gate.

"I have to get back to first class," I said.

"Everyone down here tells me that," the officer answered. "You won't be going anywhere." With that, he fastened the gate with a padlock and hurried up the stairway.

9

My first reaction was disbelief. I tried to shake the gate loose, but it didn't budge. It was much too high to climb. The padlock was secure. I was shut away from the rest of the world. For a couple of minutes I stared through the gate at the stairs that would have taken me to safety, and then I turned and walked slowly back down the corridor and past the cabins with their frightening sounds of distress. I was surely walking toward my death. Now that I believed I would never see it, England seemed very pleasant. I thought of my mother and how terrible the loss of her only remaining child would be and how it would serve Father right for sending me away. I realized I was taking comfort in feeling sorry for myself.

I passed a cubbyhole of a stateroom with no one in it. Probably its occupants were among the scores of patients in the room that had been converted into a hospital. I was so anxious to crawl into a safe corner that I gave no thought to germs which might be lurking in the stateroom, but only crept inside and closed the door, thinking I would hide from the disease. The room was full of reminders of its occupants. There was a neatly folded red *sari*. Red was a bride's color, so perhaps a young girl was going to an arranged marriage in England with a young Indian man. I saw as well another *sari* of a more ordinary cloth and children's sandals in several sizes, so the bride must be sharing her room with another woman and that woman's children. They were all sick, maybe dead.

I realized how dangerous the room might be. The sickness, like a menacing beast, overcame them and even now might be lurking in the cabin, ready to attack me. I flung open the door and fled down the hallway to Mrs. Blodget.

When she saw me, she put her hands over her face as if to shut off the sight of me. When she took away her hands, there were tears in her eyes. "Rosalind, what are you doing here? What am I to say to your parents? They trusted me."

I explained about the gate. At once she rushed over to an officer who was overseeing everything and began to plead with him. "She has only been here for a few minutes. She can't be contagious."

He looked unhappy, and I could see he wanted to let me go, but he was under orders. "I have instructions from the captain, and I cannot make an exception. If I made an exception, there would be a mutiny from all the other people down here who want to get away. She should have thought what she was doing."

As if she could protect me from what was all around me, Mrs. Blodget put her arms about me and drew me close. I breathed in the smell of disinfectant and strong soap. "What will your parents think of me?" she said. "I have failed them. Indeed I have." She paused and cocked her head, listening. Then she brightened. "William has pointed out that all things are ordained and you were meant to be a help to these poor people."

I looked about at the rows of suffering patients stretched out on the soiled cots. They were groaning and calling out. I felt completely helpless. Worse. They disgusted me. William could not have been more mistaken. Hastily I said, "I don't know anything about nursing."

"Never mind about the nursing. Cholera creates a terrible thirst. You can carry water to the patients, but you must wear these gloves and this mask."

There were pitiful cries for water all about me. An Indian boy no more than eleven or twelve years old lay nearby, and I filled a cup and helped him to swallow. "What's your name?" I asked.

"Ravi," he whispered. He was burning with fever. I remembered how Amina used to wring out a cloth in cold water and lay it on Mother's forehead when she had one of her headaches. I found a napkin, soaked it in a basin of water, and laid it on Ravi's forehead. He looked up at me with a smile so faint it was like the writing on a blackboard that was not completely erased. I went from bed to bed giving sips of water and trying to speak comforting words that, as I looked at the dying patients, seemed like lies.

In the moments when he brightened a little and could talk, Ravi told me he was traveling to London, where he would be going to school. "I will study Greek and Latin. I have a scholarship to the school, so I must not die."

"Is your family with you, Ravi?" I asked.

"No, no," he said in a weak voice, "the cost is too great." He gave a great sigh. His eyelids, with their fringe of black lashes, fluttered, and Ravi fell into a restless sleep. Another time he said, "I wonder how the other boys will like me?" And still later, when he was feeling a bit better, he said, "I didn't want to come, but my father said I must learn how to talk and act like a British gentleman so that I can get a good job in our country and bring honor to our family."

To make conversation I asked, "What is the name of your school?" For he seemed more alert as he talked of his future.

"Westminster School," he said, and pride strengthened his voice a little.

"Westminster School! That's where my brother went."

"And was he happy there?" Ravi asked.

How could I tell him, ill as he was, that my brother had died at that school? "Yes," I said. "Yes, he was very happy." It was not entirely a lie. Edward's letters had been full of talk of how homesick he was, but there were also stories of friends he had made and successes at cricket.

I kept returning to Ravi, thinking that even if I should become sick and die, a thought that terrified me and made my hands tremble, if I could help to save Ravi's life, it would help make up for what had happened to my brother.

By the end of the day, as the patients became familiar

to me, I lost my disgust and a little of my fear. The two nurses seemed to accept me, paying me no attention, but one of the two doctors came to examine a patient just as I was holding a cup to the patient's lips. In a gruff voice the doctor asked, "Where did you come from?"

I explained.

"I'd send you away if I could, but you have to be treated like anyone else. You would be safer off in a corner by yourself rather than moving about exposing yourself to the sick people."

"I don't mind," I said. "I'm in no more danger than you are."

The gruffness left his voice. "Good girl," he said. "We'll get through this." He moved on to another bed, but his words had made me strangely happy.

At the end of the day Ravi was less feverish and even ate the bit of rice I fed him, but I could barely stand. Mrs. Blodget came to fetch me. "I have scoured out one of the empty cabins with a solution of carbolic acid. We'll have a bite to eat, and then I'll tuck you in and get a bit of rest myself."

I barely had the strength to lift a fork and wanted only to lie down. I slept in my clothes, stumbling onto my bunk

and thinking only of blessed sleep. When I awoke sometime in the middle of the night, I looked over and saw
that Mrs. Blodget's bed was empty. "William is after her," I
thought, and turned on my side and closed my eyes, glad
he had let me be.

Each day was much the same. After a moment of surprise upon awakening to find that we were still alive and
well, Mrs. Blodget and I had a breakfast of tea and toast
with the nurses and doctors and the staff of the ship who
were on duty. We donned our masks and gloves and went
to the hospital room and our patients. There were a few
empty cots now. Like Ravi, some of the patients were well
enough to recuperate in their cabins. Other empty cots
were a reminder of patients who had died and with only a
bit of ceremony and a few prayers had been dropped over
the railing of the ship into the ocean to join all the invis-
ible creatures lurking beneath the sea's surface.

Death was new to me. Edward's loss was always there,
but I only felt it from a distance. Of course there had been
death all about me in India, where Indian children died,
their illness often untreated, but those deaths had not
touched me. The closest I had come to death was in nature,
like when I found a parakeet lying on the grass one day.

When I picked up the still-warm, limp body and held it in my hand, I saw that all its bright colors had faded, and I saw how much was lost when something dies. I said as much to Mrs. Blodget that evening as we prepared for bed.

"Yes, the psalm says, that we are 'a wind that passeth away, and cometh not again.' But what doesn't die is the love we give to others. There is no end to that."

I thought of Mother and how she feasted on the memories of affection Edward had shown her in his letters. I recalled the trouble I had given Father. I wished I had shown him more love so that he would have better memories of me if I died.

I had come to know some of the patients that were slipped into the sea. There was an elderly Indian man who shook his head at the cups of water I tried to give him and mouthed the word *sannyasa*. When I asked Mrs. Blodget about this, she said, "He is telling you he has reached the state of renunciation. He has given up all worldly things and death will be a release, perhaps into *moska,* the union of his soul with Brahma and an end to the many lives of reincarnation."

"But what will happen to him then? Will he go to a kind of Brahman heaven?"

"No. You simply disappear into nothingness. Of course, we don't like the sound of it—our version of heaven is quite different—but the Hindus tire of reincarnation, of always coming back as one thing or another, and welcome rest."

It was hardest to get used to the deaths of the children I had nursed. There were two sisters with long plaited black hair and terrified looks on their faces. They pleaded to be next to each other, and I had one of the cots moved so they could be side by side. As long as they had the strength to do it, they held hands. They died within minutes of each other. We were never able to find the girls' mother, but when they were carried out to be buried, Mrs. Blodget and I begged that they be buried together and we stood there as the small black package fell into the sea.

There were happy recoveries as well. A mother and father and their three children were reunited and built a little shrine to the goddess Shiva, begging candles and flowers from the ship's servants who brought us our food. Many of the people who had recovered prayed at the shrine, and some went there to weep.

When at last we reached Southampton, most of the cots were empty and we were alive. Mrs. Blodget and I, along with all the people in steerage, were quarantined and not allowed to leave the ship until a medical team boarded the boat and examined us. Then it was an endless two days more before we could get our things from our cabin and leave the ship for the train to London. Mrs. Blodget was too tired to make her way to the third-class car and suffered the luxury of first class. By dinnertime, however, she had regained enough strength to visit third class, and when she returned she said, "That boy you cared for, Ravi, is on the train. He seems a nice chap, but who would send their child thousands of miles away by himself at so tender an age and into a world about which he knows absolutely nothing?"

I thought I could ask the same question of myself.

10

Mrs. Blodget and I walked down the gangplank into the arms of my Aunt Ethyl and Aunt Louise, who had taken the train from London to Southampton to meet me. I had seen photographs of them, but there had been no color in the pictures. Aunt Ethyl in person was still mostly black and white and gray. Her black hair was tightly combed away from her face and knotted into a muffin-like knob in back. Her skin was a pale white, as if she had been locked indoors for years, and the wool suit that covered her from neck to ankles was the gray of a stormy day. Aunt Louise had the same black hair, but wisps and curls had escaped her muffin. Her complexion was the same parchment color as her sister's, and her suit was the color of burnt bacon. Both wore gray velvet toques, hats like inverted ice cream cones with feathers stuck in them. Aunt Louise nearly suffocated me with her warm embrace. Aunt Ethyl was cautious in her handling of me, so that her greeting was more avoidance than welcome.

When my aunts had arrived to meet us, they had been told we were not among the passengers departing the ship because we had been exposed to cholera and were quarantined with other third-class passengers. They had become distraught, so when at last they saw us alive and well, Aunt Louise wept with relief and Aunt Ethyl began to scold Mrs. Blodget.

"What were you doing in steerage? Rosalind's parents paid for her to travel first class on the ship. I suppose you exchanged the first-class passage for third class and pocketed the money, putting Rosalind's life in peril."

At once I began to explain. "It wasn't like that at all. We had a first-class cabin, but William told Mrs. Blodget to go down to help the people in third class who were ill, and she did. Later, when I went down, I wasn't allowed back up."

With great suspicion Aunt Ethyl asked, "Who is William?"

"William is my husband," Mrs. Blodget said.

"A man traveled with you!" Aunt Ethyl appeared even more upset.

"William is dead," I assured her. "He just keeps in touch."

Hurriedly Aunt Louise said, "I am sure Mrs. Blodget did all she could to care for Rosalind, and what matters is that she is here and safe."

Before my aunts could lead me away, I threw my arms around Mrs. Blodget and promised I would not forget her. "Or William," I added. It was the last I was to see of her, but sometimes faced with a choice I thought of her and of William and what he would have done, and he always turned out to be right, though following his advice was never easy.

For the first time in my life I was in my native land, but I had no time to look about. There was a bustle of activity to transfer my baggage to the train that would take us to London. A porter helped us onto the train, and Aunt Ethyl found a compartment. There was very little conversation, for a single man and a couple were in our compartment and it appeared that Aunt Ethyl thought it undignified to display one's business before strangers. When Aunt Louise urged me to tell about the events of our shipboard passage, Aunt Ethyl interrupted her with a curt "That can wait until we get home, Louise."

In no time the train was pulling into Victoria Station, and I stepped into the city of London. My first impression was one of noise: the whoosh and roar of the train station and then the street with its noisy taxis and buses. It was afternoon, but I couldn't find the sun in all the murky soup of sky. There was a quickness to what everyone did that I wasn't used to. Compared with the leisurely ceremony of India, it seemed graceless.

In the taxi Aunt Ethyl kept a suspicious eye on the meter while Aunt Louise pointed out the sights. "There is Westminster Abbey," she said, "and there is the Thames River and the Houses of Parliament." And there they were. I forgot all about my sorrow at leaving home and the strangeness of a new country. The pictures I had seen in history books were coming alive. It wouldn't have surprised me to see King George V and the Princess Royal strolling about. The taxi turned onto Lord North Street, a narrow street of brick homes. It pulled up to one of the smaller houses, number 23, an address familiar from the letters I had addressed and received over the years. Aunt

Ethyl extracted from her pocketbook a little leather change purse. She unsnapped it and counted out some coins for the driver, who received them with no comment and not much pleasure.

The three-story house sat between two larger homes like a child with a parent on either side. The entrance was into a dark passageway that I learned later led to a kitchen and scullery. A stairway took us to a hallway. On the right was a dining room, and on the left a large sitting room. There were three bedrooms on the third floor. I was led at once to my room, where I found a narrow bed with a plain white spread, an oak dresser with a small mirror, a washstand, and a straight chair with a floor lamp beside it. A window looked out on brick houses across the street. On the wall was a framed painting of a country church and graveyard. There was also a little desk with a vase holding a bouquet of roses. Everything I needed was there, but except for the roses, nothing more.

Aunt Ethyl marched into the room and adjusted the curtains with a snap of her fingers. She frowned. "Louise, those look like the Petersons' roses."

"Oh, they won't mind. They're away on vacation just now, and it's a pity to let the flowers go to waste.

Rosalind's room looked so bare. I wanted it to look welcoming. Surely we should have spent some of the money our sister sent for us, to make the room more comfortable."

"Nonsense. I'm sure Cecelia would not have money wasted." Quickly she turned to me. "You will want to change, Rosalind. Dinner is promptly at six o'clock. Come away now, Louise." She gave her sister a little push and ushered her toward the door. I saw Aunt Louise pause for a moment and stand firmly where she was, like a stubborn puppy, but she must have thought better of it, for she followed her sister out, pausing only to smile at me as she left—a disappointed smile, as if she were missing a treat that had been promised her.

The ship with its many Indian passengers had a connection with home. Now home and India were thousands of miles away. I squeezed my eyes shut and tried to conjure up a picture of my room in India, with its bedspread and curtains made of brightly colored Indian cloth. I thought of the comfortable chairs and the soft pillows and, most of all, the view of a garden lit with sun and full of flowers. The room I was shut into seemed more punishment than welcome.

I put on a silk dress with a lace collar. I had to make the best of living with my aunts, and I thought dinner was where I would start. Aunt Louise said, "Rosalind, how lovely you look."

Aunt Ethyl said, "We are very simple here. There is no need to get yourself up."

Our meal was truly simple and very white. There was a white cream soup, a stewed whitefish served with white potatoes and boiled white cauliflower, and for desert a white pudding that had no taste at all but for the strawberry jam that had been spooned over it.

Aunt Ethyl frowned at the jam. "Louise, the pudding would have been quite enough without the jam."

"Just this once," Aunt Louise said. "To celebrate Rosalind's being with us." She turned to me. "I suppose you are used to a more adventurous cuisine."

"Usually we had English food," I said, "but sometimes our cook would make us a curry or *tandoori* chicken, and when I was in the bazaar I would have *chapatis* and *samosas*."

"You ate street food?" Aunt Ethyl asked.

"Well, Isha knew the best places."

"Isha is not an English name."

I tried to explain to Aunt Ethyl. "Isha was my *ayah*'s daughter, and we're the same age so we were raised together. She's expecting a baby."

"A baby! At fifteen. A very peculiar friend. What can your parents have been thinking."

"Well, of course she's married, to Aziz. He works in the bazaar, and he's a member of the Congress Party."

Aunt Ethyl dropped her spoon and stared at me. "If you have such peculiar friends, it is no wonder your parents sent you to England."

"What is the Congress Party?" Aunt Louise asked.

"It's a party that wants India's independence from England," I answered.

"Nonsense! It is nothing of the kind." Aunt Ethyl glared at me. "It is a group of traitors disloyal to Great Britain, who has cared all these years for the Indian people, who cannot care for themselves."

In a very low voice Aunt Louise said, "Perhaps the Indian people have not had a chance to care for themselves."

I was amazed to see that Aunt Louise had tears in her eyes. At first I was surprised to find she cared so much for the Indian people when she had never been to India or, as

Gloria Whelan

far as I knew, even met an Indian person. But then I saw she was speaking not of India but of herself. In the short time I had been with them I had seen how Aunt Ethyl bullied Aunt Louise, and I guessed it had been like that all her life. I couldn't help saying, "I believe all people long for their independence."

Aunt Louise gave me a grateful look, but Aunt Ethyl said, "You are talking of something about which you are ignorant. I don't want to hear the Congress Party mentioned again in this house. I believe your parents sent you to England to get you away from such evil influences."

I felt I had been foolish to speak so openly when I had no idea how my aunts felt about India, and I resolved to keep my opinions to myself. Hastily I changed the subject. "When will I start school?" I asked, for I was already anxious to find a way to leave my aunts' gloomy house and see more of London.

"I have arranged for you to begin at Miss Mumford's school this coming Monday."

"Oh, sister," Aunt Louise said, "I thought she would be attending St. Martin-in-the-Fields on Charing Cross Road. Rosalind's father was very clear that he wanted the best for her, and he did send such a sum of money. And

Miss Mumford has only the one teacher besides herself and no Latin."

"You need not concern yourself with Rosalind's schooling, Louise, and there is no need for her to learn Latin. What possible good can it do her when she returns to India? Miss Mumford will teach her useful things."

Aunt Louise would not give in. "I had a great deal of pleasure reading Virgil, Ethyl. Of course, I am a bit rusty now, but I still pick up the *Aeneid* and read about poor Dido and how she loved Aeneas. It's so beautifully tragic."

While my aunts were quibbling, I was dealing with my disappointment in having to go to an inferior school when the one thing that consoled me about having to leave India was the promise of an excellent education. Also, I was surprised to find that my Aunt Louise curled up with a Latin book for amusement. I had dismissed her as a bit of a foolish woman, but now I saw that I had not formed my own opinion of her but taken my Aunt Ethyl's view. I resolved not to do that again. I think it was the moment when I began to side with Aunt Louise against Aunt Ethyl in what I could see was an old war. I recalled what my mother had said about Aunt Louise having been in love and how Aunt Ethyl had put an end to the romance to keep Aunt Louise from marrying and leaving her. No wonder Aunt Louise returned over and over in her reading to a tragic love story.

The pudding was eaten and tea served. Aunt Ethyl passed the sugar bowl to Aunt Louise but hung on to it so that when Aunt Louise reached for a second cube of sugar, the bowl was snatched away. "I have told you, Louise," Aunt Ethyl said, "so much sugar cannot be good for you."

Aunt Louise said nothing, but I saw the look in her eye, and I was sure that there were times when she rebelled against her sister. At least, I hoped so, and I also hoped I would be there to see it.

After our dinner, we settled in the sitting room. Aunt Ethyl stabbed at some embroidery in shades of poisonous greens, and Aunt Louise showed me photographs in family albums. There were pictures of my mother and her two sisters in long curls, butterfly bows in their hair, long white dresses, black stockings, and black-laced boots. Mother usually stood protectively beside Aunt Louise while Aunt Ethyl stood a little aside, regarding the two younger girls with a critical look. There were some pages where I noticed pictures had been removed. When I inquired, Aunt Louise looked quickly at her sister as if she were waiting to see what Aunt Ethyl would say. When Aunt Ethyl refused to look up from her embroidery, Aunt Louise quickly turned the pages. It was only later, when I was alone, that it occurred to me that the photographs might have been of my brother, Edward.

As album followed album and page followed page I swallowed my yawns and tried not to fall asleep. I was just about to make an excuse to escape to my room and my bed when there was a stirring outside. Somewhere in the neighborhood, doors were opening and closing. There were footsteps and voices. Aunt Louise got up and ran to the door, ignoring her sister's order. "Louise, come back here at once."

From the open door Aunt Louise called, "Come here, Rosalind. You must not miss this."

I knew I should have stayed put, that there would be reproach if I ran to the door, but I couldn't help myself. And besides, I was happy to see Aunt Ethyl disobeyed. Black-suited men in bowler hats were emerging from doorways. They disappeared into the dark street, then passed through a pool of light from a streetlamp only to vanish once again. "What is it?"

"The division bell," Aunt Louise said. "Parliament is

meeting, as they often do in the evenings, and they are about to have a vote. Many of the members of Parliament have returned home for a late supper or on some business. Because they are within walking distance of Parliament, a bell rings in their homes to let them know about the vote. Division they call it, the two sides divided. I love to stand by the door and see the members on their way to decide great questions of state, decisions that may change the course of nations."

We heard Aunt Ethyl's angry words. "I won't have you peering out the doorway in that fashion. What will people think? Come in at once."

Still we lingered until the last dark figure turned the corner. As Aunt Louise reluctantly closed the door I decided there was a division going on in this house as well as in Parliament, and my vote was for Aunt Louise.

Alone in my room that night, everything seemed strange. The sound of cars in the street instead of the chirping of crickets, heavy fog that shut out the stars, the warm blanket at the foot of the bed that told me cold nights were coming. In India we spoke of England as home, but now that I was here, England seemed a foreign land. I closed my eyes and thought of more familiar nights, nights in which curtains were stirred by warm breezes and outside my window the fish owl hooted in the jacaranda tree and in the distance the jackals howled. Some memories were already difficult to recall and I worried that in another year they might be gone altogether.

11

There was a week before the fall term began at Miss Mumford's. "Let me show Rosalind about the city," Aunt Louise begged.

Reluctantly, Aunt Ethyl gave her permission. Aunt Louise asked in an embarrassed voice if she could have a little spending money. "We might stop for a cup of tea, and there will be taxis."

"There is plenty to see within walking distance of our home, Louise, and as for tea, you can have all the tea you wish right here." No money exchanged hands. I considered it very degrading that a grown woman should have to beg for a shilling, and I understood the sacrifice Aunt

Louise had made in sending me my Christmas shilling.

We set out right after breakfast. "There is a sign of autumn," Aunt Louise said, pointing to the swaths of bark shed by the plane trees. "And I have noticed the martins are flocking. I do hate to see winter come. My walks are so cold, and they are my one amusement." I had a vision of her shivering in the cold and snow of a winter day to escape Aunt Ethyl, and I thought I would make the same choice.

In a sad voice Aunt Louise said, "Many years ago, Rosy, I took your brother, Edward, on a tour of London. Of course, he was just a small boy, so our trip was a short one, but how he enjoyed it all. The sadness of his death is with me every day, as I know it is with your dear mother. I cannot help but feel responsible, for he was under our care. One day I will take you to little Edward's grave and we will do our mourning there, but for today I mustn't let unhappy memories spoil what I hope will be a pleasant adventure.

Of course I had seen my mother and father's unhappiness over Edward's death, but now I realized that Aunt Louise and Aunt Ethyl would have sad memories as well, for Edward had been with them when he died. I wondered why Aunt

Louise would say she felt responsible, and I resolved one day when I knew my aunts better to ask about the circumstances of Edward's death. Now, I saw, was not the time. Aunt Louise was determined to make this day a happy one for me.

We walked first to Westminster Abbey. I had seen a print of the Abbey on the wall of the club, so I knew it was very grand, but I was not prepared for its size and splendor. Aunt Louise, in her role as tour leader, said, "Originally, it was the church of the Benedictine monks who lived here in 600 B.C. It is where the kings and queens of England are crowned and many of them buried." After we had wandered among the marble columns and stained-glass windows and bent our necks to look up at the soaring ceiling, Aunt Louise led me to the sepulchre of Queen Elizabeth. "Not one of my favorites," she said. "So demanding, so controlling." She moved on to the sepulchre of Queen Mary of Scots. "Elizabeth kept her cousin, Mary, imprisoned for eighteen years and then had her beheaded."

We wandered through Poets' Corner, where there were names I recognized: Thackeray, Chaucer, Tennyson, Milton, Scott, and the Brownings. "You know the story, I am sure," she said, "of how Elizabeth Barrett escaped her domineering father to marry Robert Browning." Aunt

Louise moved on, pausing at the grave of a name I did not recognize, William Wilberforce. "A man to be admired," she said. "He led the battle against slavery."

With a shy smile she said, "You must not tell Ethyl, but I have this fantasy of the kings and queens and poets and famous men all coming alive at night and mingling. What a sight that would be."

As we left the Abbey we passed St. Margaret's Church, and I remembered Mother telling me how Aunt Louise had engaged that very church for her wedding before Aunt Ethyl had put an end to it. I glanced at my aunt, but she was staring straight ahead.

"Next we will visit the Houses of Parliament," she said, "so that you can see where the men we saw last night were headed. The building started out as a palace. Although it is thousands of miles away, India is ruled from here. The flag flies when Parliament is sitting." Aunt Louise pointed to one of the towers. "That is the Victoria Tower, and that's the Clock Tower with Big Ben."

"Is that the clock we hear chiming the hours?"

"Yes. It has been chiming since 1859. There is an inscription in Latin on the clock that says, 'O Lord, save our Queen Victoria the First.' Isn't that lovely?" She pointed to a place on the roof. "Legend has it that Oliver Cromwell's body was dug up from its grave and hung right there in chains for twenty-five years until it was blown down in a storm and the head knocked loose. The head was passed from person to person until it was lost and then found again. I believe some gentleman has it now."

"Poor Mr. Cromwell."

"Not at all. He was a very strict Puritan, always telling people what to do. Old Ironsides, he was called. He had poor King Charles I executed, and he killed ever so many of the Irish."

We went down Birdcage Walk, along St. James Park, where we stopped by a pond and Aunt Louise extracted some toast she had saved from breakfast to feed the ducks. Again she said, "Don't tell Ethyl." It seemed the rule of her life. Yet I sensed an extra pleasure in the feeding of the ducks, as if she took an especial pleasure in doing what her sister forbade.

At the end of the park was Buckingham Palace, where George V lived. I wanted to show that I knew something of British history and said, "He came to India, Aunt Louise, and people said he wanted a better life for the Indian people."

"That may be, but some say he is a very strict parent."

Aunt Louise could talk of nothing but despots. There was Queen Elizabeth, who had imprisoned and executed Queen Mary. There was Elizabeth Barrett Browning, who escaped her domineering father. Even King George was accused of being a strict parent. I guessed she was thinking of the way she was bullied by Aunt Ethyl. The only hero had been the man who abolished slavery. I decided I would be that person for Aunt Louise, so when she said, "Perhaps we should be getting back. Ethyl will wonder where we are," I pleaded to walk a little farther, and she was quick to agree. We strolled up Constitution Hill to the entrance of Hyde Park. Traffic surged around us, and I noticed a crowd had gathered.

"Speaker's Corner," Aunt Louise said when I asked about the crowd. "They come every day to hear speakers who stand upon a box and exhort the people about some cause or other. It's a tradition here that people may say what they like at the Corner."

I thought it would be a good lesson for Aunt Louise, and in my new role as liberator I took her arm and pulled her toward the crowd. A young man was standing upon a wooden box and giving an impassioned speech about freedom for India. It was Max.

I waved my arms at him, causing him to pause for a moment and grin at me, but then he went on with his speech.

"Surely you don't know that young man!" Aunt Louise appeared distressed.

"Yes. It's Max Nelson."

"You must come away at once." Yet she didn't move, and I saw that her curiosity had been piqued.

"Max is perfectly respectable," I assured her. "He was a lieutenant in my father's regiment, and his parents are very wealthy and have a huge house. His mother, Mrs. Nelson, runs an orphanage where my baby, Nadi, is."

"Your baby!"

"Well, not really *my* baby, but one I rescued from being sold."

"Sold!"

"Yes. I'll tell you all about it sometime when Aunt Ethyl is isn't there. Anyhow, Max is going to Cambridge to study. Let's listen to what he is saying, and then I'll introduce you."

"I really think we must leave at once. What would

Ethyl say?" And yet she did not leave, and I saw that she was pleased to be doing something a little daring, something of which her sister would never approve.

"She'll never know. Please, Aunt Louise, I couldn't bear not to talk to him."

My aunt looked about as if Aunt Ethyl might be watching, and then with an almost wicked gleam in her eye she moved closer, the better to hear.

Max was finishing his speech. "And so in conclusion I insist that you look into your own hearts and ask yourself if you would consent to live as Indians must, under the heel of an occupying power. Hundreds of thousands of Indian men have fought and died in battle for England. How can we reward their bravery by telling them they are not good enough to rule their own country? That is a disgrace!"

There were several cries of "Hear! Hear!" and a shout of "Bolshie!"

Max stepped down from the box and made his way toward us. "Rosalind! And this must be one of your aunts."

"It's Aunt Louise, Max. When are you off to school?"

"In a few days. The sooner I go, the sooner I will be

finished. The only way I can endure a year in this cold country is to promise myself that at the end of that time I will be sailing for India. Now, you must promise to come and hear Sarojini speak. She is here from India. She's a good friend of Gandhi's, and she's a poet as well. She'll be speaking day after tomorrow night at London Hall on Victoria Street, and you can bring your aunts. You mustn't miss her. I'll look for you. Now I must bash off. I'm helping to make arrangements for her talk, tickets, chairs, and all that. You *will* come."

At once Aunt Louise said, "Impossible," and I said, "Of course."

Max laughed. "If I know Rosalind, she'll be there." He hurried away, and Aunt Louise pulled me in the direction of home. "Promise me you won't tell Ethyl about this."

"Yes, of course I promise, but I don't see the harm." I thought that if I was not going to learn history at the inferior school Aunt Ethyl was sending me to, I must learn it where I could find it.

But I did see the harm that evening, when at supper, with no mention of what had happened that afternoon, I asked Aunt Ethyl if I might go to a lecture the night after next.

"At night? What is the subject of the lecture?"

"A famous Indian woman, Sarojini, is giving a talk on freedom for India."

"I wouldn't hear of you going to London Hall and mingling with hundreds of people you don't know, and I can't believe you would sit still for a woman who proposes to give freedom to natives who are as helpless to care for themselves as a room full of infants."

"Aunt, that's not true. The Indian people run the trains and are in the civil service, and their civilization existed a thousand years before England took it over."

"Hundreds of thousands of Indian soldiers fought with British soldiers in the war," Aunt Louise said.

Aunt Ethyl turned on her. "Where did you hear that? You know nothing of such things, and I am appalled that you should utter such treasonous talk as that in front of Rosalind. I want no more words on the subject from either of you."

The evening went by slowly. Aunt Ethyl read aloud to us in a plodding voice Tennyson's "The Lady of Shalott," which is about a woman who has been cursed and can't look directly out at the world but rather sees the world as shadows in a mirror.

"Or when the moon was overhead,
Came two young lovers lately wed;
'I am half sick of shadows,' said
The Lady of Shalott."

I saw Aunt Louise brush a tear from her eye. When finally I escaped to my room, I was awake until the early hours planning how I should get to the lecture.

In the morning the three of us set out to buy clothes for me. We did not go to Liberty of London, which Mother often spoke of as her favorite shop, or any of the stores on Regent or Oxford streets, which I had heard spoken of by women in the club. Instead, Aunt Ethyl led us down a narrow road to a little dressmaking shop. Aunt Louise protested. "Rosalind's father sent a very large sum of money, Ethyl. Surely she should have something nicer than anything Mrs. Stringly might make."

"If Rosalind's father wishes to waste money unnecessarily, that is his business. I see no reason to encourage it."

Mrs. Stringly was formed like a sofa cushion. She had a tape measure draped around her neck and a pincushion fastened to her wrist. Scissors peeked out of the pocket of her dress. "Ah, the Miss Hartleys," she said, "and this must be the young niece you spoke of. Are we to fit her out for the London season?"

Aunt Ethyl was all business. "Two worsted dresses for school and a warm coat will do."

"I have some Scottish wool twill that just came in. You can feel it yourself, and it has lovely drape to it."

"How much?"

Upon hearing the price, Aunt Ethyl said, "The girl is probably growing, and there is no need to spend that kind of money on clothes that have to be replaced. What is this?" She was looking at a ghastly gray material of a thin weave.

Mrs. Stringly shrugged. "That is just fabric left over from some uniforms I was engaged to make for Snaresbrook, the infant orphan asylum."

"That will do. And make the hems deep. Now for a coat."

"I have a nice thick fleece. It would protect against the strongest winds."

"There is no need to be too concerned about the weather. The walk to the school is a short one. Did you make coats for the orphans?"

Mrs. Stringly sighed and reached for a bolt of dirty brown wool.

All the while, Aunt Louise was watching what was going on. Several times I saw her open her mouth as if to protest, but then she lost her courage. Now she took a deep breath. "Ethyl, Rosalind is not used to the cold winters. Should she take a chill in so thin a coat, Harlan and Cecelia would hold us responsible."

Aunt Ethyl flushed a deep red, as if Aunt Louise had conveyed to her some blame that went beyond the making of my coat. "Very well. You may use the fleece for the coat, Mrs. Stringly."

On our way home Aunt Louise looked longingly at the tearooms as we passed them, but Aunt Ethyl headed directly for Lord North Street, where we dined on shepherd's pie with a great deal of potato, but little meat.

After lunch, Ethyl went up to her room for her afternoon nap, and Aunt Louise said, "Let me show you my favorite spot."

Just a block away was Smith Square, where there was a small garden surrounded by elegant homes like a row of stylish ladies. Across the square was a church.

"St. John's Church," Aunt Louise said. "They have musical evenings there. I believe there is one tomorrow night. A fine organist is giving a Bach recital. If you think you would like to hear it, I'll ask Ethyl if we might attend. She seldom objects, since the recitals are close to home and no attendance fee is asked."

I knew little about Bach, and organ music gave me a toothache, but I quickly said, "Oh, let's. I would love to," for it would get us out of the house, and the hall where Sarojini was speaking was only a few blocks away. As we sat companionably together in the little park among the trees and the beds of bright flowers and the houses standing watch around us I dared to ask Aunt Louise, "Can you ever do as you like?"

"As I like? Whatever do you mean, Rosalind?"

I took a deep breath. "I mean, you're a grown-up, and you are always asking Aunt Ethyl for permission. I suppose she has all the money and you are dependent on her."

"Oh, indeed no. Father left the estate in equal shares to all of us, but I leave the care of the funds to Ethyl. I have no head for figures."

"You don't know how much money you have?"

She blushed. "Please don't tell Ethyl or she would feel I was checking up on her, but I did peek at my account a few months ago and I have a very great deal, but what would I spend it on?"

"Isn't there anything you would like? Isn't there anything you would want to spend your money on?"

There was a long silence. A busy red squirrel loosened a leaf, and the leaf fell into Aunt Louise's lap. She held it in her hand, examining it as if she had never seen a leaf before. At last she said, "There is one thing I long for, but you must not breathe a word to your aunt. Your mother writes such lovely letters about India. Ethyl throws them away, and I rescue them. I have them all. I read and reread them. I close my eyes and see all the bright colors. I would give anything to see India before I die."

"You have the money to pay your passage, though, and just think of all the good things your money could do in India. It was your shilling that let me buy a baby and save his life." I told her all about Nadi. At first I could see from her shocked expression she didn't believe me or didn't want to believe me, but I must have convinced her, for she said, "And to think it was my shilling. Oh, Rosy, nothing has ever made me happier."

"Come back with me, Aunt Louise. Mother would love to have you."

Aunt Louise gave me a look of such longing, but in seconds I saw the longing fade and the frightened and intimidated look I was used to take its place. "I wouldn't dare," she said, and then she asked, "Do you really think such a thing would be possible?" Before I could encourage her, she got up from the bench. "It's time we were home. Ethyl will be looking for us."

And she was. "Where have you been?" she demanded of Aunt Louise.

"We were in Smith Square. It was such a lovely afternoon."

"I can't think why the two of you would want to sit out in public for everyone to see."

"It's really quite private there, Ethyl, with all the trees and shrubbery, and it's just across the street from St. John's, so it's quite safe."

"The church is having a recital tomorrow night, Aunt Ethyl," I said. "Aunt Louise and I would like to go, and it's free."

"Perhaps I'll go with you."

Before I could think of a way to discourage her, Aunt Louise said, "That would be lovely, dear."

After dinner, we gathered as we had the evening before in the sitting room. Aunt Ethyl was about to open the book of Tennyson's poems when I said, "Why don't I tell you a little about life in India?" I wanted Aunt Louise to hear more about the country she longed to see.

Before Aunt Ethyl could stop me, I said, "Diwali is next month. It's a sort of Hindu Christmas with five days of celebration. I always know it's coming, because the servants turn out their houses and scrub everything, and then they open all their windows so that Lakshmi, the goddess of wealth, can come into their homes. The women put on their best *saris* and make delicious dinners, and my friend Isha sneaks me some of the things her mother makes, like almond *katli* and *soan papdi*. Everyone gives everyone else sweets and gifts. At night there are little clay lamps everywhere, as if all the stars have fallen down from the sky to light the city. Isha says the lights are a celebration of our inner light, our true nature. Isn't that beautiful?" The more I rattled on, the more real India was becoming in my mind. I could see vividly all I was describing, and it seemed awful that I should be deprived of Diwali. I brushed away a tear so that my aunts would not see it.

Aunt Louise was leaning forward, listening intently. I was sure she was imagining herself there to experience it all. Aunt Ethyl's face was very red. "What you are describing is a pagan festival, surely not a proper celebration for a Christian." She opened Tennyson and began to read in a voice that killed all the words.

That night, Aunt Louise followed me to my room. "I don't think I can bear to die without seeing India," she whispered, and then disappeared into the dark hallway.

12

All the next day I worried that Aunt Ethyl would go with us to the lecture and we would not get to hear Sarojini. In the morning I found my aunts in aprons and busy on the yearly duty of dusting the books in the library. I offered to help and was given an apron. The books had belonged to my grandparents. My grandfather must have had a deep interest in battles, for there were books on the Franco-Prussian war, the American Civil War, the first Boer War, even the Trojan War. There were books on gunboats and catapults, fortifications, sieges, and armor. On the walls were very old muskets and crossbows.

When I asked if Grandfather had been a belligerent

man, Aunt Louise said, "Oh, no, he was the most gentle man you could imagine. Anyone could get round him, until you went a bit too far. Then there was war and no one could defeat him."

I wondered if under Aunt Louise's gentle behavior, like her father's, there lurked some limit, if one day she would have her own war with Aunt Ethyl. I hoped I was there when it happened, so I could enlist on her side.

As the time for the recital drew near, the sky darkened and there were drops of rain on the window. "No need to venture out on a night like this," Aunt Ethyl said, "I certainly won't."

Hastily, I said, "Oh, I don't mind the rain at all. We have monsoons in India, and it rains for months. You never stay home. You just go. You don't mind, Aunt Louise, do you?"

"Not at all. I've been looking forward to it. It will be so nice to have someone with me."

Aunt Ethyl insisted we put on our Wellingtons and trench coats, but no sooner were we out-of-doors than the downpour gentled into a shower, making us smile at each another in all our rain gear. When we reached St. John's Church, I put my hand on Aunt Louise's arm. "I have to go to hear the Indian woman talk. You heard Max say she was a friend of Gandhi's. I must hear what she has to say."

"Oh, Rosalind, you can't. What would Ethyl say!"

I started off. "I promise I'll be back here before the recital is over."

Then, just as I guessed she would, Aunt Louise said in an almost eager voice, "I couldn't possibly let you go alone. I'm coming with you."

Murmuring all the while about what Aunt Ethyl would do if she found out, Aunt Louise hurried along beside me. When we reached the hall and she saw the crowd, a look of excitement came over her face. "I don't believe I have ever attended a lecture like this." And then in a worried voice she asked, "Why are there policemen here?"

"I'm sure it's just to contain the crowds. Let's sit right up close, up where we can see her." As I pushed past people I looked for Max and finally spied him in one of the front rows. He saw us at the same time and waved us over. There were two empty chairs next to him.

"You made it. I knew you would, and how excellent to have brought your aunt. All the newspapers are here. Her lecture will be on the front pages tomorrow. Parliament is discussing some sort of home rule for India, so this will add fuel to the fire."

A wave of excitement went through the audience as a gentleman led Sarojini onto the stage. I had thought she would look romantic and impressive; instead she looked rather like a typical Indian housewife. In his introduction the gentleman said Sarojini had been a brilliant scholar both in India and then in England. When she was fifteen, just the age I was, she had fallen deeply in love with an Indian doctor and married him. At the same time, she began to write poems, but most of her life had been spent urging self-government for India and working for women's emancipation.

Her voice, when she began to talk, was certainly not the voice of a housewife. I felt she was taking me by the hand and looking in my eyes, with no one else there, wanting to tell me something that would make all the difference in the world to me. She told of the people who were killed in the terrible massacre at the Golden Temple of Amritsar, how those people had come to celebrate the harvest and the Sikh New Year and they had been trapped by the walls that surrounded the park and fired upon by British soldiers. "I tell their stories," she said, "because as Gandhi says, truth needs to be repeated as long as there is someone who disbelieves it."

The whole hall was absolutely silent. Aunt Louise's

hand clutched mine. "There has been violence on both sides," Sarojini said, "but such violence must stop. Gandhi says, 'The force of love and pity is infinitely greater than the force of arms.' We must listen to him."

She said she was not speaking for self-government for self-government's sake. "Gandhi says in India we have three million people who have to be satisfied with one meal a day, and that meal consists of a *chapati* containing no fat in it and a pinch of salt. He tells us we must adjust our wants, and even undergo voluntary starvation in order that those three million may be nursed, fed, and clothed. That can be accomplished only when India is free. That is what Gandhi says, and that is what I say."

Everyone sprang up to give her a standing ovation, and no one applauded with more enthusiasm than Aunt Louise. "Oh, Rosalind, I do believe this is the most exciting night of my life. No. I believe it is the *only* exciting night of my life." She turned to Max. "Young man, I want to thank you." She reached into her pocketbook and emptied out the few coins that were inside. "Give this to Sarojini. It's very little, but it's something."

There were people in the hall pushing toward the stage to get closer to Sarojini. As we turned to leave we came face-to-face with photographers snapping pictures of her as she stood behind us on the stage, the flashes of their cameras momentarily blinding us. Max ushered us out of the hall and offered to walk us home. Aunt Louise thanked him, but she knew as well as I did that there would be questions if we arrived at Lord North Street in the company of a young man. When I took Max's hand to say good-bye, he bent over me and kissed me lightly on the cheek. "I'll write to you," he said, and hurried away. I stole a look at Aunt Louise. She must have been thinking of her own lost love, for she brushed a tear from her eye.

On the walk home Aunt Louise said over and over, "Something must be done. Yes, something must be done." She was like a fire that had been kindled. When we were almost at our door, she said, "I know what I will do."

Before I could ask what she meant, the front door swung open and Aunt Ethyl greeted us with a sharp "Where have you been? Surely the recital could not have lasted so long."

Aunt Louise paid no attention to the question. Instead she worked her way out of her Wellingtons, shed her coat, and faced Aunt Ethyl.

"Ethyl, I want a checkbook for my own money."

"Nonsense. Whatever put that idea in your head?"

"I do have a considerable sum of my own money, do I not?"

"That may be, but if you have need of money, you may ask me."

"No, Ethyl, I will have my own checkbook, and I will go tomorrow to see our solicitor to have the arrangements made." With that, she kissed me and bid us good night.

I gave Aunt Ethyl a quick glance. Her face was very red and her features were all squinched up, as if someone had let the air out of her head. Hastily, I said "Good night" and followed Aunt Louise up the stairway. In my excitement over the way she had stood up to her sister, I lay awake as Big Ben chimed the hours. When I finally drifted off to sleep, I dreamed that Aunt Louise was chasing Aunt Ethyl around my grandfather's library with one of his muskets.

I slept later than usual and was awakened by angry voices. I quickly dressed, praying that Aunt Louise would be able to stand up to her sister, but when I hurried down the stairway and into the sitting room I found Aunt Louise crumpled among the cushions of the sofa. A furious Aunt Ethyl turned on me. "I took you in, Rosalind, out of the kindness of my heart, and this is the thanks I get. You have betrayed my trust and led my poor, stupid sister into a treasonous plot against our nation."

I backed away from the force of her words, which were like so many poisonous arrows. "I don't know what you mean."

She thrust a newspaper at me. It was the London *Times,* and there on the front page was the headline INDIAN REBEL INCITES CROWD TO END BRITISH GOVERNMENT OF INDIA. Beneath the words was a picture of Sarojini, and in the forefront of the picture stood Max, me, and Aunt Louise.

"You have been a viper in our bosom," Aunt Ethyl said. "No wonder Louise has lost her senses. There can be no question now of allowing someone so easily led to handle her own money."

All my plans for Aunt Louise's transformation from worm to butterfly were dashed. Instead of setting her free, I had made it impossible for her ever to lead her own life. Aunt Ethyl was saying, "I shall write to your parents today, Rosalind, to tell them of your mischief. It's time they know what an evil child they have, one who consorts with terrorists."

I should have kept quiet, but I couldn't. "Sarojini isn't a terrorist. She believes, like Gandhi, in nonviolence."

"Don't you dare answer me back. You know nothing of such things. You need a reformatory, not a school. You will remain in your room today, and I will have your breakfast sent up."

Reluctantly, I left the room and headed for the stairway, when the sound of Aunt Louise's angry voice stopped me. Perhaps she would fight after all. I listened at the door.

Aunt Louise said, "If you write to our sister, Ethyl, I will write to her as well. I will tell her about Edward."

I had no idea what she meant and held my breath waiting for Aunt Ethyl's anger. Instead, there was no word from Aunt Ethyl.

In the same accusing voice Aunt Louise went on, "I will tell our sister how the school let us know how ill little Edward was and that they asked if we wanted to send a specialist. I found a doctor who would have gone at once to treat Edward, but you said his fee was too high. You wouldn't even let me see the child. You let him die uncomforted and alone, and then you told our sister the school had not let us know until it was too late."

"You're lying."

"No, I'm not lying. I have the letter from the school. I'm glad Rosalind took me to the lecture last night. I am glad to find people in the world who care about other people and who are willing to make sacrifices for the less fortunate. I don't know much about history or governments, but I understand what it is to have someone dictate to you, to control your every move. I understand India's wish for freedom."

The door flung open, and a red-faced Aunt Ethyl stalked out of the room. She appeared startled to see me, but she said nothing, only brushing by me and ascending the stairway as if it were a mountain.

Aunt Louise came out and took my hand. "Oh, Rosy, it was wrong of you to eavesdrop. I didn't mean for you to hear what I said. You must put it out of your mind at once. Come, we'll have breakfast together."

Neither Aunt Louise nor I had an appetite. There was tearing of the toast into small pieces and pushing a spoon around to make tracks in the oatmeal, but there was little eating. "Was all that true about Edward?" I asked.

"Yes. Those were the worst days of my life, Rosalind. I had to send the sad news to my sister knowing secretly in my heart that we could have done more to help dear Edward. I don't say we could have saved his life, but I say we could have done more. Of course I have no intention of ever telling all that to your poor mother. It would break her heart. But let Ethyl think so, let her confront her conscience. Now, would you like to accompany me to my solicitor?"

My aunts' solicitor, Mr. Thorston, was a dumpling of a man with a chubby, round face that was mostly pursed lips and squinty eyes like a cherry and two raisins in a bun. He welcomed my aunt with much enthusiasm. "Miss Hartley, at last! I haven't set eyes on you since your dear father's death and the reading of the will. I was beginning to think you were a figment of my imagination. And this is your niece all the way from India. What a charming girl. How pleased you must be to have her with you. Sit down, ladies, and tell me what I may do for you. I feel quite the chivalrous knight."

My aunt grasped her pocketbook with both hands, as if she needed something to hang on to. "Mr. Thorston, in the past my sister has been kind enough to take care of my financial affairs; consequently, I know very little of them."

"That is a pity, Miss Hartley. Financial affairs are not the dull thing some would have them. I have spent my adult life among financial affairs, and I have not had a dull moment. Every day I arrange the affairs of my clients, like you and your sister, so that their money grows, just as the leaves on a tree grow. With me it is always springtime, for the leaves are always increasing. Then it is the turn of my clients to take those lovely green leaves and use them to bring joy to themselves and others."

"That is very interesting, Mr. Thorston. What I wanted to ask is whether or not I have sufficient money for my purposes in my account."

"Sufficient! Ah, that depends on what your purposes are, dear Miss Hartley. If you wish to buy a castle or a pail of diamonds, I would say what you have is not sufficient. But should you wish to buy a nice house or a new wardrobe or a modest sailboat or even all three of those things, then I would say your funds are sufficient. Your sister is of a different mind than mine. In caring for her money and for yours she has been prudent—no, more than prudent, she has been frugal. Where others would have spent, she has skimped. Therefore, your tree is overloaded with leaves. I hope you have come here this morning with the idea of giving yourself the pleasure of making use of what I have strived to accumulate for you."

"Yes, that is exactly why I have come. I would like a checkbook, Mr. Thorston, and after this I will have the care of my own money."

"Not only the care, dear Miss Hartley, but I hope the pleasure as well."

He reached into his desk and extracted a checkbook, which he handed to Aunt Louise. He then opened a large ledger and smiled his great smile as he turned over the pages. "Yes, just as I expected, you are a very warm person." He smiled at me. "We say that, Miss James, to describe someone like your aunt, whose tree is full of leaves."

After saying good-bye to Mr. Thorston, I accompanied my aunt to the bank. We stood at a little counter, where she prepared to write her first check. Her hand trembled as she took up the pen. "Rosalind, you must assist me."

I wrote out the date and the sum, and Aunt Louise signed it. She took it to the teller, and I could see from the hesitant way she handed her check to the man and the delight with which she received, with no problem, a sheaf of pound notes, that right up to that moment she had not really expected to be in possession of her own money.

We had taken a bus into the financial section of the city, but now, outside the bank, Aunt Louise, with many false starts, raised a tentative hand and signaled for a taxi. She had the taxi wait while she went into a florist's for a bouquet of lilies, and then she directed the driver to take us along the Fulham Road to the Brompton Cemetery, where we got out of the taxi and made our way through a gate, past a chapel, and down a long path.

"At last, Rosy, you shall see where your dear brother is buried." We walked across the long stripes of shadows made by sun shining on ancient trees. Marble angels looked down on us, and squirrels scampered out of our way. Aunt Louise stopped to listen to a songbird. "A thrush," she said.

At last we came to a grassy mound. A simple headstone read, EDWARD GEOFFREY NICHOLAS JAMES, 1893–1904. It was the closest I had ever been to my brother. I wanted to tell him all about Mother and Father and me and my aunts. I wanted to know him. I ran my hand over the grass. It was as close as I would ever come to my brother. Aunt Louise laid the lilies on the grave. I saw her turn her face from me, and I knew she was crying. I put my arms around her, and we held each other. Then we turned and walked back the way we had come.

It was early afternoon when we returned home. We had stopped for luncheon on Regent Street. "My mother used to take us here for lunch," Aunt Louise had said. "I've always wanted to come back, but Ethyl frowns on eating out."

It was wonderful to see how proudly she gave her order to the waitress and how she marveled over the tiny cucumber sandwiches and smoked salmon and the little dessert cakes with their pastel frosting. I wished Mr. Thorston could see how she was enjoying some of the green leaves from her tree. But Aunt Louise had no intention of spending all her leaves on little luxuries.

"Tomorrow," she said, "you will help me find where in India my money will do the most good."

Aunt Louise could not bring herself to drive up to the house in a taxi, so she had us dropped off at the end of the street. I had hoped that we could slip up to our rooms without seeing Aunt Ethyl, but she was at the door waiting for us, a cablegram in her hand.

13

"I don't know where you have been, but your outing has kept you from urgent news." With that, she thrust the cablegram at me.

> GET PASSAGE FOR ROSALIND'S RETURN
> TO INDIA SOONEST. LETTER FOLLOWS.
> HARLAN JAMES.

My first happiness at the thought of returning home was gone. Could Father's change of heart mean that Mother was unwell? Maybe even dying? And I was thousands of miles away. The terse words did nothing to reassure me.

Aunt Ethyl snatched the cablegram from my hands. "What can your father be thinking? Are you a package to be sent back and forth across the ocean? He must be mad. Nevertheless, I would be less than honest if I did not say it is for the best. I have tried in every way I know to provide you with a proper home, and how have you rewarded me? You have created nothing but havoc since you have been here. I no longer know my own sister. I will not be sorry to see you leave, so that we may return to the peaceful life we had before you came."

As relieved as I was at the thought of going home, I worried over why I was being sent for, and I cringed under the whip of Aunt Ethyl's words. But now that I was escaping I could be humble. "I'm truly sorry," I said. "I didn't mean to be such a trouble." I looked at Aunt Louise, hoping she would stand up for me, but she was looking down at the floor, her shoulders caved in, clutching her pocketbook as if at any moment her sister would tear it out of her hands.

Aunt Ethyl said, "After receiving your father's cable, I discovered there is a ship sailing for Bombay in a week. I will go this afternoon and book passage for you as your father wishes. Now I want to see you in my study at once, Louise."

I stood there, helpless, as Aunt Louise followed her sister into the study like a trained puppy. Aunt Ethyl closed the study door with a sound like a thunderclap. I hurried to my room, trying to put my new world together. There was nothing I wanted more than to return home, but thinking about Mother, I fell into misery. It was impossible to stay in my room.

I hurried out, turning down one street and up another, not thinking where I was going but only wanting to walk away from my worry. Wandering down Great College Street, I saw a collection of ancient stone and brick buildings. In the background were the towers of Westminster Abbey. There was a kind of garden with benches, and on one of the benches a boy was sitting. I was sure he was an Indian. I wanted to run up to him and tell him that I was going home. He must have felt me staring at him, for he turned to look at me and I saw that it was Ravi.

"Rosalind, what are you doing here?" He made room for me on the bench.

"I'm staying nearby at my aunts'. What are *you* doing here?"

"This is my school, Westminster."

"Ravi, I'm going back home. I've just heard from my father. I'm worried that my mother might be ill, but I'm so happy to be leaving here."

"You are lucky. I hate it here. Some of the boys call me a wog behind my back."

"That's terrible."

"It's not all bad. I have a good tutor, and I'm learning science, which I wasn't learning in India. If I don't starve to death, I'll survive."

"Starve? Don't they feed you?"

"They feed us, but I am a Hindu and can't eat beef, and our dinners have huge slabs of cow, or stews with beef."

I heard Mrs. Blodget's William talking to me, and with no thoughts of what Aunt Ethyl would say I quickly asked, "Do you get any time off? You could come to my aunts' for dinner. I'll get the cook to make chicken." I paused. "Can you eat chicken?"

"My family is not strict, so chicken is fine. It is the sacred cow I cannot touch."

"When can you come? It must be soon, because I'll be leaving."

"We have Sunday afternoon off. I'd have to get permission, but I could explain about your aunts, and I am sure they would let me go."

Ravi took me about, showing me the school. In spite of his complaints, he was proud of everything and even suffered the hoots and catcalls of some of the other students who saw him walking with me. Before I left him, I gave him directions to our house.

Seeing Ravi made me feel my journey home had already started, which made it seem I was that much closer to Mother.

It was dinnertime when I got back to Lord North Street. Aunt Louise was alone in the sitting room. Whatever Aunt Ethyl had said to her had turned her into her old timid and apologetic self. "I can see why Ethyl would be angry with me, Rosalind. All these years she has done her best for me. I've been ungrateful."

"Nonsense. You're a grown woman. You have a right to live your life the way you want to. You can't let her tell you what to do. You were so happy today. Think of the fun we had."

She burst into tears. "I'm not brave like you are. Once you are gone, I'll never have the courage to speak out again. I think if you were going to be here, I might have a chance, but now it's hopeless."

Without thinking, I said, "Then come with me."

She grabbed my hands. "When I can't sleep at night, I imagine getting on a steamship, and then I imagine the whole cruise and how I would arrive in India and your mother and father and you, Rosalind, would be there to greet me and how you would all take me about, and I imagine all the wondrous things I would see." She heaved so great a sigh that I felt it like a warm breeze blowing over me.

"You have the money, and you can do what you want. Why can't you go back to India with me?"

Aunt Louise dropped my hands and refused to look at me. "Ethyl made me give her my checkbook. She locked it in the desk drawer."

"Aunt Louise, how could you let her! Never mind. We'll get it back. In the meantime you'll have a chance to meet an Indian right here in your own house. He's coming on Sunday to have dinner with us. I met him on the boat when he was sick and nearly died, and now he's here in school and he's a Hindu and can't eat meat, and that's just about all he gets, so I invited him and I'm going to get Rita to make chicken for him."

Aunt Louise's eyes brightened, and there was excitement

in her voice. "What a lovely idea, Rosalind. We'll go and talk with Rita now."

Rita was not only the cook, she also dusted the furniture, carried hot water upstairs for our baths, and cleaned the ashes from the fireplaces. We found her in the kitchen, where she didn't like company. If she'd had her way, she would have had a dragon at the door. You could always tell what mood she was in by the way her apron strings were tied. If she was in a good mood, there was a sort of butterfly bow. If she was in a bad mood, there was an angry knot. Today the strings were tied in a limp and stingy bow. Not a good sign, but not hopeless.

"Rita," Aunt Louise asked, "could we have chicken for our Sunday dinner?"

"Certainly not. We always have a roast of beef. You know that."

I said, "We're having a guest who can't eat beef."

"Nonsense. Everyone can eat beef." She thought for a minute. "Have they got trouble with their teeth?"

It was a natural question, because Rita's teeth were more often seen in a glass on the sink than in her mouth. When Aunt Ethyl scolded her, she would grumble under her breath, "If I was paid a decent wage, I could get some teeth that fit."

Before I could explain that it was a boy my age, Aunt Louise quickly said, "Yes, that's it. He has a terrible time with his teeth. Chewing beef is agony to him. A little chicken would be just the thing."

"Poor old soul," Rita said. "I'll stew it nice and tender and serve it with a healthful salad with the lettuces all cut up fine, and for dessert we'll have a nourishing custard that will just slip down his throat."

"That's very kind of you," my aunt said. "I'm sure he will appreciate it."

As we left the kitchen Aunt Louise said, "We must tell Ethyl you have invited a guest. She must be prepared."

We found her in the sitting room occupied in mending a pair of her stockings. She hastily put them away, as if they were too intimate a garment to be seen publicly. Saying nothing about what had just happened in the kitchen, I settled across from her, wondering how I could manage to explain Ravi's visit, but she gave me no chance. Instead she said, "Perhaps I was a little hard in what I said, Rosalind. I would not want you to suggest to your parents that your stay here has been unpleasant. Of course we have been pleased to have you with us for even such a short visit. Now that you will be returning, perhaps there is something you would like to see or do in the few days remaining to you."

Of course Aunt Ethyl would not want me to describe to my parents how unjust she had been to me, how she had hoarded the money they had sent for my clothes, and how she had arranged to send me to an inferior, inexpensive school. "There is one thing, Aunt Ethyl. On the ship on my way over I met a young boy from India who was going to Westminster School. I happened to be walking by the school this afternoon and I saw him. He's very lonesome and anxious for a good meal. He has Sunday afternoon off, and I invited him for dinner. Is that all right?" I held my breath.

"You should have spoken to me first, Rosalind. The invitation ought to have come from me. However, many of the boys from the homes of cabinet ministers and profes-sional men go to Westminster. I suppose his father is high in the British government, one of the men sent to rule in India." She gave me a sharp look. "How old is this boy?"

I guessed she suspected me of some flirtation. "He's just twelve," I said.

"Well, then, since this will be your last Sunday with us, he may come."

I didn't dare look at Aunt Louise, but I humbly thanked Aunt Ethyl.

The next days were spent making arrangements for my passage. Father's letters had come, one for me and one for Aunt Ethyl. Mine filled me with worry over my mother and an eagerness to be home with her.

Dear Rosy,

Your Aunt Ethyl's letter telling us of the cholera epidemic on board the steamship and your involvement and quarantine was a terrible shock from which your mother is still recovering. I have had to send for Dr. Morton, who is advising rest for her palpitations. In my concern for her health I am doing the best I can to accede to her wishes, however inappropriate, understanding she is beside herself with worry. I know she will have no peace until you are here with us, and I have promised her that I will ask your aunts to send you home at once.

Of course I regret the loss to your education. I will undertake to teach you myself and will find a competent tutor to supplement my efforts. I am guessing that this will be good news to you, for I saw how much you regretted leaving India. I hope you will return with increased maturity and greater good sense.

We _both_ miss you, Rosy.

Love,
Father

After reading her own letter from Father, Aunt Ethyl said, "Your father wants you to travel first class. I will have to rebook the passage. A great waste of money, if you ask me."

There was nothing I wanted more than to be with Mother and in India. Father had told me how German and English airplanes had fought one another during the war. I wished there were such airplanes as that to carry people across oceans. I did not see how I could stand all those days aboard a ship.

I read again the words about Mother's illness and couldn't help blaming Aunt Ethyl, so I asked, "Aunt Ethyl, why did you write my parents about what happened on the ship? You must have known how they would worry."

"I hope you are not pretending to instruct me on my responsibilities, Rosalind. Your parents had a right to know. As it turns out the result suits us all. I have not felt that you are happy here, and I cannot have someone disrupting our life as you have done. My sister has not been herself."

Aunt Ethyl was talking as if Aunt Louise were not there. I glanced over at her to let her know I was on her side, but she would not look at me. I hated to think of leaving her. I guessed what the rest of her life would be like, being ground under her sister's heel like an insect. I couldn't bear it, and the first moment I was alone with her I begged her to come with me, but she only shook her head. "It's not to be, Rosalind. I haven't the courage."

In all the excitement I had nearly forgotten Ravi, but when Sunday came I was in the kitchen supervising the chicken. "Rita, haven't you got any coriander or cumin seeds or some garlic and red pepper?" I remembered the lovely smells from Isha's house when she was preparing *tandoori* chicken for Aziz.

"I never heard of such things. Garlic is for foreigners, and why would I be putting red pepper in the poor old soul's food? No doubt he has a sensitive stomach at his age, as well as poor teeth."

I had to be satisfied that it was chicken and not cow.

Ravi was on time and looked very handsome in a dark suit, white shirt, and pink-striped school tie. I had been hovering at the door looking for him, and I immediately led him into the sitting room, where Aunt Ethyl and Aunt Louise, in their Sunday church dresses, were prepared to welcome him. I had expected Aunt Ethyl would be a bit surprised that Ravi was an Indian and wondered if I should have warned her, but I wasn't prepared for her shocked look or her inability to say a word.

Aunt Louise jumped up and hurried over to take Ravi's hand and lead him to a comfortable chair. "I'm Louise Hartley, and this is my sister Ethyl. We are both so pleased to have you with us. I understand from Rosalind that you had a very narrow escape from the cholera."

"Yes, ma'am. I think I survived because Rosalind took such good care of me. She's an excellent nurse."

I asked Ravi about school, and he said, "Oh, it's Greek from morning to night. I am learning everything about the ancient world—the Trojans and the Peloponnesians and Athens and Syracuse and why Oedipus put out his eyes."

"Don't you find the Greek language very difficult?" Aunt Louise asked.

"Well, it's better to learn it than to have your ears pulled or your hand hit with a ruler."

"Do you miss India, Ravi?" I asked.

"Yes, every minute, but I tell myself I must keep busy and the time will pass. Today, because of your kindness, I don't miss it so much."

Ravi had a natural courtesy and seemed comfortable in this strange home. Aunt Louise's warm welcome and my chatter covered up Aunt Ethyl's stiff silence. Perhaps he thought there was something wrong with her that kept her from speaking, because from time to time he smiled at her and included her in his conversation, which only made Aunt Ethyl redder and angrier.

When Rita came in to announce dinner, she looked about, blinking at Ravi. "Dinner is ready. Where is your guest?"

"He is right here, Rita," Aunt Louise said, and indicated Ravi.

Unlike Aunt Ethyl, Rita quickly covered her surprise and said to Ravi, "If I'd known it was a young boy with a boy's appetite, I would have had a proper joint of beef instead of chicken."

Ravi didn't look disappointed at all.

Aunt Ethyl led us into the dining room and seated herself in her accustomed place at the head of the table, looking as if she were going to preside over some frightful thing like an execution. Aunt Louise indicated a chair for Ravi and seated herself at the other end of the table while I sat down across from Ravi. In her first words to Ravi, Aunt Ethyl said, "Who are your parents, boy?"

"His name is Ravi, Aunt," I said, but she paid me no attention.

Ravi looked a little surprised that Aunt Ethyl could actually speak, but he said politely, "My father is a solicitor, Miss Hartley. He helped Gandhiji in his fight against the Rowlatt Act."

"What is the Rowlatt Act?"

"It is a very unfair thing done by the British, Miss Hartley. It says you can imprison someone without a trial."

"Your father is against the British government!"

"No, ma'am. We Indians have all learned the blessings given to us by the British. In my school in India I had to list them on my examination paper. I can still recite them: public health, law and order, schools, roads, irrigation works, bridges, telegraphs, and railways. But in the Rowlatt Act and in other things the British gave us injustice as well. My father is against injustice." Ravi smiled politely and dug into his chicken with enthusiasm.

Aunt Ethyl pushed back her chair and stood up, her napkin dropping to the floor. "I will not sit at the table with someone who associates himself with treason against the British government." With that, she stamped out of the room.

Ravi looked from me to Aunt Louise. "Ought I to go away?" He looked reluctantly at the chicken still on his plate.

Hastily, Aunt Louise said, "No, indeed. You will excuse my sister. I am sure that in India as well you have people who are not quite rational."

Ravi looked relieved. "Oh, yes, Miss Hartley, they are called holy fools and are greatly revered. It is believed God has paid them special attention. You are fortunate to have so spiritual and virtuous a person in your home."

"Yes, Ravi," Aunt Louise said, "we can hardly be thankful enough."

Without being asked, Rita brought in a serving platter and watched with satisfaction as Ravi piled more chicken onto his plate. When the time for dessert came, she saw that he had a very large helping of pudding.

With Aunt Ethyl no longer there to inhibit her, Aunt Louise chattered away at Ravi, asking a thousand questions about India. "Have you seen the Taj Mahal? The Golden Temple of Amritsar? The Ganges River? The houseboats in Kashmir? The Agra Fort?"

Ravi had to admit that he had never been far from Bombay. "But I went with my parents just outside the city to the island of Elephanta to see the caves. Carved into the rock of the caves are magnificent temples with pillars and statues, all done fifteen hundred years ago."

When he saw how interested Aunt Louise was, and perhaps because he was a little homesick and liked to talk of his city, Ravi went on to tell of the pleasures of Bombay. He described Ganesh Chaturthi, the holiday when everyone took their statues of Ganesh, the elephant-headed deity, to the seashore. "We pack our lunches and our bathing suits, and we take our statues of Ganesh down to the sea and drown them!"

"And why do you do that?"

"Parvati was the wife of Shiva, and when Shiva was away at war, Parvati needed someone to guard her door while she bathed, and so she made a son, Ganesh, out of sandalwood paste. He was to guard her door, but when Shiva returned, the son did not recognize Shiva and wouldn't let him in, and that made Shiva angry and he cut off Ganesh's head. Parvati was very angry, and to pacify her Shiva got the head of an elephant for her and put it on the body of the son he had slain, and Parvati breathed life into it and was very happy with her new son."

"My, what a story!"

Ravi was encouraged by Aunt Louise's rapt attention and kept on telling stories and legends. The afternoon passed so quickly that Ravi, seeing the time, said he would have to hurry back to the school. He thanked us both and even thought to go into the kitchen to thank Rita, who pronounced him a "real little gentleman with a fine set of teeth."

When she heard the front door close, Aunt Ethyl came down the stairway, taking each step as if it had to be stamped on and killed. "You are a most irresponsible girl," she said to me. "I can't think why you invited that boy into this house."

Before I could say a word in my defense, Aunt Louise said, "I thought he was a very nice young man, and I thought you were very rude to him, Ethyl."

Instead of flying into a rage, Aunt Ethyl flung herself onto a chair and commenced a fit of tears, whereupon Aunt Louise hastily apologized. I saw that Aunt Ethyl knew more than one way to control her sister.

Nothing more was said about Ravi, but after we went upstairs for the night I heard a timid knock on my door, and there was Aunt Louise in her wrapper, her hair loose about her shoulders and without her glasses, looking younger and prettier. She held a knife, and her hand shook.

"Rosalind, I have broken into Ethyl's desk and retrieved my checkbook. Will you come with me tomorrow morning to book my passage on the steamship you are taking to India? I believe I will need moral support."

"Yes, yes, of course I will." And I hugged her.

Making some excuse about my wanting to take home Mother's favorite perfume, which wasn't available in India,

Aunt Louise and I hurried off immediately after breakfast, wanting to leave before Aunt Ethyl went into the study to find the checkbook gone.

First we went to the bank, where Aunt Louise withdrew a generous sum of money, and then to the steamship office, where I produced my ticket with its cabin location. Aunt Louise was given a nearby cabin. On the way to purchase her train ticket, she kept opening her pocketbook and looking to see that the ticket for the ship was still there. From the train station we went on to Liberty of London, a large timbered building that looked like something medieval but was really a department store. "I wouldn't want your mother to be ashamed of me, Rosalind. None of my clothes are suitable for the Indian climate."

Aunt Louise moved about in Liberty in the same way Isha and I wandered in the bazaar, relishing everything but buying nothing. She put her hand greedily on a dress and then took her hand away as if the dress might burn her. I knew she saw her sister looking over her shoulder, frowning, forbidding. At last we came to a silk dress printed all over in bright flowers. "Millefleur," she whispered.

"What is that?" I asked.

"It is a print called 'a thousand flowers.' It is just the way I think of India."

She bought three of that same dress in different patterns. After her first purchase, the others came easily, and at the end of the day it took the two of us to carry all the packages.

There was the question of how her purchases were to be spirited into the house without being seen, and I hit on the idea of buying a length of cord, which Aunt Louise hid in her pocketbook. I stood under her window with the packages while she went upstairs and dropped the cord out her window. I fastened the cord to each package, and Aunt Louise pulled them up one by one.

I was glad to hide the ugly clothes Aunt Ethyl had bought me under my bed, leaving room to pack Aunt Louise's things in my suitcase. She had a great deal of difficulty deciding what she would take and what she would leave, but in the end she took only her new clothes, a sad little bundle of pictures, her mother's pearls, and a pincushion my own mother had made for her when they were both girls.

There was a bad moment that evening. Aunt Ethyl spent most of her spare hours knitting socks for orphans in an institution she supported. From time to time Aunt Louise was called on to hold her hands out to help in the winding of the yarn from the skein into a ball. When she had performed her usual duty, I watched how her mouth drooped and her eyes teared. I was sure she was wondering who would be there to perform the task after she left, and, indeed, the idea of Aunt Ethyl sitting alone in that big house was daunting. On an impulse I asked, "Would you like to visit India one day, Aunt Ethyl?"

"I am perfectly content where I am, Rosalind. Why would I want to cross the ocean to see what could not possibly compare with my own country?"

I believe the smugness of the answer relieved Aunt Louise, for she sighed a large sigh and a look of relief came over her face, the look of someone who has just escaped a great danger.

In the morning a taxi took my aunts and me to Victoria Station and the train. Aunt Louise was in her usual brown serge suit, which was shiny at the elbows and seat. While Aunt Ethyl was busy paying the taxi and hailing a porter to carry off my luggage, I kept an eye on Aunt Louise, who was unusually silent and preoccupied. She turned to me and whispered, "I'm losing my courage." I grasped her arm to keep her close.

When it came time to board the train, Aunt Louise threw her arms around Aunt Ethyl, knocking off her hat, which always looked as if it had been clapped on with a mallet. "Louise!" she cried. "Have you lost your mind?" She pushed at Aunt Louise and untangled herself, as if Aunt Louise were a python intent on squeezing her to death.

"Good-bye, Aunt Ethyl. Thank you for everything. I'll be sure to write." I headed for the train, pulling at Aunt Louise, who was like a fish that wouldn't be reeled in. She opened her pocketbook and extracted an envelope, which she thrust at her sister. For a moment Aunt Louise stood there, trying to find words. When the words did not come, she turned away and followed me onto the train.

As the train pulled out I watched Aunt Ethyl from the window of our compartment. She stood openmouthed on the platform, the envelope clutched in her hand. Aunt Louise wouldn't look and was crying into an already-sodden handkerchief. I gave her a fresh one and tried to console her, but the sobs kept coming, as if she had years and years of tears saved up and was at last getting rid of them.

It was only when we were well out of London and the porter came through with his announcement of first seating for dinner that Aunt Louise dried her eyes. "It is such a treat to eat on a train," she said. "I always thought it extraordinary that you could sit at a table and have dinner while the countryside flew by. Let's go at once, shall we?" She blew her nose and headed out into the corridor.

In the dining car Aunt Louise reached across the table and took my hand. "I would never have had the courage to leave without your support, Rosy. I really think you were an angel sent to deliver me. I do feel guilty when I think of my sister alone, but inch by inch I was suffocating." She sat up very straight. "Perhaps I shall be punished for leaving Ethyl, but for now I mean to enjoy myself."

She looked greedily out the window at the scenery and then turned to smile at the passengers at the table across from us and at those in the tables on either side of us, as if they were all guests at her party. She ordered her dinner from the little menu card in a clear voice that faltered only a little among the many choices. When the dinner was over and our dessert of *omelette aux confitures,* which turned out to be a jam omelet, had been eaten, the waiter brought our tea. With great ceremony Aunt Louise dropped three cubes of sugar into her cup.

As I watched her put the cup to her lips I thought Aunt Ethyl had, at last, been swallowed up in a sip of sweetened tea.

15

Unlike Mrs. Blodget, who had had William looking over her shoulder, Aunt Louise showed no guilt over her first-class accommodations on the ship. The farther she traveled from Aunt Ethyl, the more she escaped her sister's begrudging ways. Shortly after boarding, we were given a cablegram from Aunt Ethyl. Aunt Louise handed it, unread, to me, as if the piece of paper were dangerous and might have the power to transport her back to London. "You look at it, Rosalind, and tell me what it says."

The message was brief.

YOU MUST BE MAD. I DEMAND YOU
LEAVE THE SHIP AT ONCE.

Had there been one word of love, one suggestion of not being able to do without her, I believe Aunt Louise would have fled the ship, but there was no such word. When I read her the message, Aunt Louise only shook her head.

She explored her room with the same wonder and excitement I had shown as a child when I had received a dollhouse for Christmas. "Just look at this, Rosalind, a little round window to look out at the ocean, my own bathroom and towels with the ship's name embroidered on them, and someone has unpacked my suitcase and hung up my clothes! And look here. There's stationery with the name of the ship and a pitcher of ice water just for me. I'd be happy to stay in this room forever."

When I called for Aunt Louise at dinnertime, I found she had changed into one of her new dresses. She held on to my hand. "Will there be strangers at our table? They will certainly think me very simple and unsophisticated. You must nudge me if I talk too much. Ethyl always did." Aunt Louise was so giddy with excitement, she had to hold on to my arm.

Seated at the table, she picked up the engraved menu card at her place and read it silently to herself, whispering to me, "It's a feast for a king." Most of the other passengers at our table were couples returning to civil service positions in

India. They were full of praise for England and complaints about all they would miss when back in India. One of the wives turned politely to Aunt Louise and asked, "I suppose you hate to leave."

"Oh, not at all. It's my first visit to India, and I am so looking forward to it. I am sure there is nothing like it."

A Colonel Brighten, who appeared to be traveling alone, took a fancy to Aunt Louise, and I was not surprised, for there was a new brightness about her and a shine in her eyes. "That's the girl," he said. "Look on life as an adventure. I could show you plenty of things in India that would amaze you."

He became attentive to Aunt Louise, showing her how to crack the claws of her lobster and urging dessert on her. "I have to watch my tummy, but you look like a breeze would blow you away. You must eat for the two of us." As we were leaving the dining room the colonel said, "The orchestra has started up in the ballroom. If your niece could spare you, might you honor me with a dance or two?"

Aunt Louise blushed and clung to me as if she had been dropped into the ocean and I was a life preserver. "Thank you so much," she murmured, "but I'm a little tired this evening."

In a disappointed voice, the colonel said, "Perhaps another evening."

We did not go directly to our cabins but instead went out onto the deck and, leaning against the ship's rail, looked out at the dark sea. "I hope I wasn't rude to that nice man," Aunt Louise said, "but it's been years since I danced. I'm not sure I would remember how, and what would Ethyl say to my dancing with a stranger?"

"But he's not a stranger, and after you sit next to him for three weeks, he *certainly* won't be. Anyhow, what Aunt Ethyl would say doesn't matter. It's what you want."

"Yes, of course I realize that, Rosalind, but I keep feeling she is beside me. I have depended on her to make my decisions for so many years that I am out of the habit of deciding for myself. It is what I admire so much in you. You seem to be able to walk right in to places where you have never been before, with your head up. If only I had your courage when I was younger, it would have changed my life."

I was not sure where my courage had brought me. I had saved Nadi, but I had been sent in disgrace to England, and now I was being summoned home and had no idea what I would find. Would I be sent to England every time

I displeased my father and then brought home to please Mother? How did you separate yourself from others who wanted to make decisions for you? Some of them, like Aunt Ethyl, might just want to control you, but others, like Father, might know more than you did and only want what was best for you. I wished that, like Mrs. Blodget, I had William with me to tell me what to do. But then, wasn't that what a conscience was for, and what if my conscience and Father's were different? When was I old enough and wise enough to listen to my own? It all made me dizzy.

Just then, the moon rose, throwing a handful of gold coins in a path across the sea. Aunt Louise put her hand on my arm. "Oh, Rosalind," she said, "if only Ethyl could see that, it might melt some of the hard places."

We were two weeks into the trip before Aunt Louise could bring herself to dance with the colonel. I was dancing, too. A lieutenant had approached me at the end of one of the dinners and introduced himself. "George Radlett," he said, and led me to the ballroom, where his style of dancing was workmanlike, as if he had learned it as you learn algebra or chemical formulas. His conversation went along the same lines. "Where do you live in India?" "What does your father do?" "Where do you go to school?" After he finished the questionnaire, he was left with nothing to say, and I had to fill the silences with all the stupid things silences bring out in people. There were none of the agreements and disagreements that made taking with Max so much fun. I did not see how I could wait a whole year for him to return to India. Making some excuse to George, I hurried to my room to write a long letter to Max spilling out all my thoughts and questions and giving, I'm afraid, a very rude description of Lieutenant Radlett.

On the morning we were to disembark I found Aunt Louise full of doubts. "What will your parents say when they actually see me walk down the gangplank with you? What if they send me back?"

We had already cabled my parents from the ship, and I reminded Aunt Louise of their answer. "They said, 'Nothing could please us more.' Of course they won't send you back. Mother will be so happy to see you. I know she loves you and has always been so sorry about your disappointment."

"Disappointment?"

I saw that I had given Mother away and stumbled on.

"Mother told me you were going to get married and Aunt Ethyl stopped you."

"Yes, that was a difficult time. I have often wondered what my life would have been like had I married the young man. Perhaps I, too, would have a daughter like you. What I am worried about now is being alone for the first time in my life. I have always depended on my sister."

"You'll have Mother and Father and me." I didn't include the colonel, but I had seen him exchange addresses with Aunt Louise the night before, and I had heard him ask permission to visit her.

Happy as I was about setting foot in India, I had my own doubts about what I was returning to. What would my life be like? What did Father mean when he said he would himself undertake my education? Did that mean he would just empty into me all that was in him and then that would be me? Or would he share his experiences with me and let me mix them in with my own thoughts?

Would I be allowed to see Mrs. Nelson and Nadi? Would Isha still want to go to the bazaar with me or would she be busy getting ready for baby? Whatever I faced, I felt I would have Aunt Louise on my side, and I thought what fun it would be to sneak off with her and to show her the bazaar.

I would see India all over again through her eyes.

Father was waiting for us when we got off the train in Calcutta. He hugged me first and then, more discreetly, Aunt Louise.

"Where is Mother? Is she all right?"

"Yes, Rosy, she has been improving ever since she knew you were returning. Frail and helpless as your mother sometimes seems, I believe she has a will of iron. She has brought you back across the ocean. All this was against my better judgment, but nonetheless, I am very happy to see you, and both your mother and I are delighted that you have brought Louise with you. Now let's be on our way. Your mother will be counting the minutes."

The monsoon rains had ended, leaving Calcutta squishy, like it needed wringing out. I was used to the dampness this time of year, but I noticed Aunt Louise delicately patting her forehead and neck with her lace hanky, and once, when she thought no one was looking, she surreptitiously fanned her long skirts to get a bit of air.

As anxious as we were to see Mother, there were delays, for as Father and I were talking, Aunt Louise was continually wandering off and had to be hunted down. Once we found her buying *dosas,* little pancakes, from a street merchant to give to a beggar child. Also, we took a brief ride about the city on the way to the train so that Aunt Louise might see something of Calcutta. The months of rains had made muddy trails of the streets. There were puddles everywhere, with small children splashing about in the dirty water. Clumps of garbage floated by, and down one flooded street I saw a man paddling a small boat. Aunt Louise nearly fell out of the taxi at the sight of a large snake swimming about in a pool in the middle of the road.

When we came to the Victoria Memorial, she begged to leave the taxi and have a quick look. Father sent me to watch over her, but I lost her in the crowd, and when at last I found her, there were tears in her eyes. She sighed, "You know, in all of her years on the throne, the queen never saw India. It would be like knowing you possessed a magnificent necklace of emeralds and rubies and never wearing it, or even taking it out to admire it a bit." But I thought it wasn't Queen Victoria she was thinking of, but herself and how much of life she had missed and the wonder that all of that had changed. She had been hungry for life, and now she was drinking it in with great gulps.

At Howrah Station, where we were to board the train that would take us home, we lost her one more time. There were peddlers everywhere selling candy, roasted chickpeas, jewelry, sandals, rugs, sugarcane, and shawls. It was a shawl that Aunt Louise insisted on buying.

"Nonsense, Louise," Father said. "The man will rob you. Wait until we get home and Cecelia will show you where to shop."

Aunt Louise seemed to agree, following us through the station, but the next time I looked she was gone. While Father fumed and guarded our luggage, I hunted through the station. But it was Aunt Louise who found me, hurrying to take my arm, a gaudy shawl of woven reds and purples draped around her shoulders. She apologized. "I felt so colorless in my brown suit, Rosalind, as if I were bringing all the drabness of home with me. I wanted to belong."

Mother was on the porch to greet us. She hugged me and then Aunt Louise and then moved back and forth between us again as if she couldn't bear to let go of either of us. Father tried to calm her, but she wouldn't be calmed. Her face was flushed with excitement, giving her a healthy look, but when we went in the house she held tightly onto my arm, needing support. Ranjit and Amina were there to welcome me home and to greet Aunt Louise.

Amina whispered to me that Mother was "very ill" after I left. "But now that you are home, all will be well." She added, "Isha will be happy to see you."

As soon as I saw that Mother was busy making Aunt Louise feel at home I hurried off to find Isha. She was in her mother-in-law's house but hastily put aside the lentils she was sorting as she looked for tiny stones, and followed me out into the garden. Her *sari* concealed her pregnancy, but her round, glowing face gave it away.

"At last Aziz's mother treats me with some respect," she said, "but she feeds me things with strange tastes to insure my baby is a boy." Isha examined me as I had examined her. "You look older," she said. "You had better get a husband before it's too late."

I told her how I had gone to the meeting for Sarojini and how my picture had been in the newspaper. "Is Aziz still working with the Congress Party and Gandhi?"

"Yes, but you must not tell. It is becoming very dangerous. There is talk of demonstrations and arrests, but I don't care about all of that. My *sass*, my mother-in-law, has promised me a new *sari*. You must come with me to the bazaar to help me choose."

We made plans to meet the next day. "I want to bring my aunt along to see the bazaar."

"Is she very rich? Maybe she will buy you the silver bracelet you like."

When I returned home, I found Mother stretched out on her chaise longue with Aunt Louise beside her. Together they were beginning to fill in the last twenty-five years of their separation, interrupting one another, crying over some things, laughing over others, Aunt Louise telling of her life with Aunt Ethyl. Several cables had come from Aunt Ethyl, all of them angry and all of them ordering Aunt Louise back.

"I shall never go back," Aunt Louise said. "If you will have me, I'll stay and make myself useful. Surely there will be something I can do in this needy country."

And there was. I could not wait to see Nadi, and the next morning, with Mother's pleading and Father's reluctant permission, Aunt Louise and I went to the orphanage. Mrs. Nelson greeted us.

"Well, Rosalind, you had an exciting time in London. I have had a long letter from Max, and he sent the very fine newspaper picture of you and your aunt." She turned to Aunt Louise and said, laughing, "I am afraid with my son and your niece you were among some very questionable company."

"How is Max?" I asked.

"He is very well and is looking forward to returning next summer. He enclosed a note for you with his letter." I put it aside to read the moment I was alone. I went with Mrs. Nelson and Aunt Louise to the nursery, where Nadi was in a high chair having a bowl of porridge. I scooped him up and tried to hold him, but he was strong now and squirmed in my arms to be let go. While I was holding a reluctant Nadi, I saw Aunt Louise put an arm around a small boy whose arms and legs were like sticks.

"A very sad story," Mrs. Nelson said. "We found him abandoned on the street. It's difficult to get him to eat, and so we must coax him to take every bite, but I don't have the help I need to do it."

"You do now," Aunt Louise said. "If you will let me, I'll come every day." She smoothed back the boy's curly hair and fed him a spoonful of porridge.

Everything was working out. I was home where I belonged. Mother, with me and Aunt Louise here, was getting well. Aunt Louise was safe from Aunt Ethyl and had found a purpose. Max would be home next summer.

I had found a moment to read Max's letter. "One of my professors," he wrote, "is against giving India its independence, and the other is all for it, so we have some fearful arguments, and I shout the loudest. I can't wait to return from exile here in this cold world. Just remember you are not to get into any mischief until I get there and can join you."

The monsoon rains were over and the air fresh-washed. As I walked up our driveway, my arm linked in Aunt Louise's, on either side of the path the pink blossoms of the oleanders were unfolding in the noon sun. I thought everything was perfect and there was nothing to worry about. Of course, all my life, when I had thought there was nothing to worry about, something always happened, and this day was no different.

Mother and Father greeted us, Mother with a worried look and Father with an angry one. Father said, "We have had a cable from Ethyl. She booked a passage to India and is on her way."

My arm was still linked with Aunt Louise's, and I felt her whole body stiffen and then relax. "Never you mind," she said. "India can surely absorb one more person. And as for me, I know who I am now."

I was startled but not worried. Aunt Ethyl would come with her coldness and her stinginess, but India would warm her against her will, and how could she be stingy when India's gifts would be all around her like a great bazaar.

Author's Note

Small Acts of Amazing Courage takes place in a river town in southeastern India. It is 1919 and World War I has been over for six months. During the war, more than a million Indian men fought alongside the British. Rosalind's father led a battalion of Indian soldiers, the Gurkha Rifles. Now that the war is over, the British in India have returned to their comfortable lives of servants and clubs.

The Indian people want their independence from Great Britain, and all across India there are demonstrations for freedom led by the Indian National Congress. The leader of the Congress is Mahatma Gandhi. Gandhi was trained as a lawyer and was outraged when the British passed legislation that allowed an Indian accused of a political act to be imprisoned without a jury trial.

He organized demonstrations against that law, but when British soldiers killed hundreds of the protesters, Gandhi chose to end the demonstrations and turned instead to the tactic of nonviolence as a means of fighting the British. He said, "Nonviolence is the greatest force at the disposal of mankind."

Gandhi's stubborn determination would be the banner under which the Indian people would finally gain their freedom.

Two things came together to make me want to write this book. The first thing is that during the years of struggle in the civil rights movement I participated in the nonviolent marches inspired by Dr. Martin Luther King Jr., who was a great admirer of Gandhi.

The second thing was a wonderful book by Vyvyen Brendon, *Children of the Raj*. It tells the story of the children of the British civil servants and army officers stationed in India. Many of those children were sent away to school in England at a very tender age. There they stayed for years with grandparents, aunts and uncles, or sometimes families that were strangers. I had just left a part of the country I loved, and I identified with their feelings of displacement and their longing for home.

I don't know how it is for other writers, but for me two things had to come together for this story to become possible—to become dimensional. It's as if I couldn't trust just one thing, but I needed the reinforcement of the second thing; as if someone was looking over my shoulder and saying, "*Now* will you believe me?" When I read about the children of the Raj, I knew I had to write *Small Acts of Amazing Courage.*

Glossary

ayah: nursemaid

bidis: hand-rolled cigarette

biwi: wife

burra mali: head servant

cholera: very infectious, often fatal disease

chota mali: assistant servant

Congress Party: politcal party founded by Gandhi and dedicated to India's freedom

dhoti: loincloth worn by some Indian men; it was made popular by Gandhi, who identified with the Indian poor

Glossary

Gurkha Rifles: Indian soldiers in the British army

havildars: noncommissioned officers

horse tonga: cab drawn by a horse.

jute: coarse fiber used for making rope and burlap

katli: an Indian sweet

kohl: powder used as an eyeliner and to darken
the eyebrows

maidan: parade ground and field for sports

Memsahib: Mrs. or mistress

Mogul: Mongol conquerors of India who ruled from the
fifteenth to the eighteenth century

monsoon: season of heavy rains in India

namaste: greeting made by holding the palms together

nimbu pani: fresh lime juice

Parliament: legislative body of Great Britain consisting
of the House of Commons and the House of Lords

Parsee: descendents of Iranian Zoroastrians who came to
India in the seventh and eighth centuries

pugree: turban

Glossary

puja: Hindu ceremony of religious worship

puris: unleavened bread

sadhu: holy man

sari: length of cloth, traditionally six yards, wrapped to make a skirt, and then draped over the shoulder and the head

sepoys: privates in the Gurkha Rifles

Sahib: mister or master

samosa: turnover with a filling

soan papdi: sweet, fried dough

solicitor: British lawyer

tabla: drum

tiffin: British term for lunch

tikka: red dot painted on the forehead to indicate the wearer is a married woman

tonga: cab to transport people through the streets

tonga-wallah: man who propels the tonga

topee: helmet, a kind of sun hat